A SEASON INTERRUPTED

Fiction/Poems/Fiction

E. C. Maxwell

For Neville 'Ned' Ross
Whose father was also
called Neville

CONTENTS

ACKNOWLEDGEMENTS

Ashton Charles, Hugh Houllier, Lennox Hyland; of Trinidad and Tobago, the late Clyde James; all that I learned, I learned from Steve Manswell; Errol Callender (in heaven so long); to these grand and noble few, the debt owed of gratitude, could never be repaid; for his graphic art, a very special thanks to Simon Alicea; to Charles Michael Smith of Harlem; to Tony Rizzo; for their unmitigated personal kindness, Leor and Mathew Sabet of the Sabet Group in New York City; James Shipman, Jaclyn Cherubini, and the remaining members of the staff at the shelter for homeless persons on Bloomfield Street, in Hoboken, New Jersey; so many others . . .

Foreword

Two of these pieces (as well as others, not included here) took shape first in Europe decades ago, during the greater part of a three-year stretch that saw me journeying mainly through Italy and France. And while for most of that period, as if in a dim-lit room, non-conversant still I remained in the languages of both countries, Italy was less constricting; I spent more time there than elsewhere, and felt always quite at home in its larger cities. I drank. The proprietress at one of the bars along the Via Brera in Milan, a diminutive, delightful (somewhat near-sighted) Albanian woman whose table, together with a few regulars, I was privileged often to share, sometimes when a dark-skinned male passed by on the street outside, would punch me between the shoulders, half inquiring, half hoping, *E Giuseppe! E Giuseppe!* I imagined that *Giuseppe,* Trinidad actor Joseph 'Junior' Iles, my good friend and (fervent in those days) partner-in-mischief, either owed her money, or that she might be enamored of him. Both assumptions turned out to be correct. And the phrase, *E Giuseppe!* 'Is [that] Joe!' was to become part of my learning experience. Helping me as I attempted to put some of this onto paper was another would-be-performer friend, Franco Zvevo. Born in Italy, of Ethiopian parents, Zvevo was the crowd favorite. With lines from *Hamlet,* his rendition of an aria from *Turandot*, God knows what else, he entertained us. Projects he managed not only in Italy, but in neighboring Switzerland and Austria as well, caused him often to travel; he made himself available always somehow still, for my thrice-monthly (free of charge) hour-long written-language guidance. These sessions hardly had begun, when he suggested that I should, purely as an exercise, compose a few short poems in Italian, which he would translate. When a few of them turned-out to be palatable, I started to get the feeling that somewhere among those stanzas, and particularly in the phrase, *E Giuseppe,* were ingredients that might one day be significant; I left Italy before anyone could get a serious look at them. Nearly thirty years had passed, when in preparation for the present work, I read the notes again. (With Joe Isles and Franco Svevo deceased, remembering of those *nessun dorma* nights, brought on a poignancy that left me all but reeling.) Some pages seemed a shambles. My Italian rudimentary remained. No more than three or four poems held together well. Here and there I reshaped a line, salvaged others, rescued a fugitive phrase; substituted, added words, deleted words—but remained true still, I felt, to the way Zvevo might have interpreted them. Surviving of all this were, *The Far;* and, of course, *Ain't That Joe*—

Sulla mattina nella citta . . .

A veteran New Yorker at the time of the 911 assaults, several winters and falls had come and gone, when no matter where in the city I happened to be, images from that morning's devastation would (as if on a stage big as life, it sometimes seemed) appear again in front of me. Not that many years earlier, when first I had arrived in the metropolitan area, I was impressed by the sight of a monument that (though yet to be finished) was on its way, I knew even then, to becoming the most memorable I ever would face. At the start of an awesome amusement-park thrill-ride that could only be breathtaking I imagined myself, so dazzlingly mountain-like and imposing the construction-complex already had become. Time went. One after the other, the seasons followed themselves. I rode the subways, ate pizza for lunch, watched as marathoners crossed a bridge; felt my way through a blackout, attended the Met, saw Shakespeare in the park; got knocked by the cops, and spent a night on Rikers Island; said goodbye to drugs and alcohol, cursed at public figures on television, lost close friends and relatives, here and there held a job—in awe every inch of the way still, of a city I had by then adopted, and came since, to love; all this from within the shadow of a colossus in the making, a network of scaffolding and dreams and jackhammers and cables and cranes; interrupting at times, even the stars and nighttime sky. Construction ended. A giant ape climbed almost into the clouds. For a wedding at the Windows on the World restaurant, a hundred and seven stories high, my name on the guest-list appeared. America's skies seemed good.

Came a September! We watched as if a David Copperfield illusion, the Twin Towers into a mound of dust and rubble turn. More than a decade later now, the fragments and fissures of that long day—its seconds and minutes and hours; its stifling moments, its glitches and gasps and warps and snares—in my memory vivid still remain. With smoke rising from the tops of buildings, my vision would blur. As I lonely walked the streets debris, seeming but a moment fallen, beside me shifting and unstable piled. The gait of a passer-by that appeared hastened, an aircraft flying low, a chorus of voices high-pitched and shrill, were signals all of distress. I would write. An essay that of questions asked, I would write! Where-from these ghosts that cry? Could any of us, a position of omniscient innocence assume? Shouldn't we all a degree of complicity shoulder? Answers, like the seasons in nature, their own time often take; seldom quick, nor full, nor easy-come. I would write. Advanced in thinking we need only be, for the dust to settle! To a system of security so thoughtfully carefully assembled we one day must wake, that not only our national posture, nor the monuments of a beloved city, nor its treasured objects and sacred sites; but more, more than the paltry demarcated areas we call homeland or countries, the here and there territories favorably aligned, the planet's surface—all of the planet's surface—will from self-aggression be protected, with the teeming everywhere millions safe, and forever finally unafraid. The smoke will clear. Of a *pramantha* with which for so long we've done nothing but scorch ourselves, the unhanding would be—should always have been—easy.

I wander the city still. On a journey asphyxiating and endless, unable at times it seems, even to breathe; to separate path from purpose, or to distinguish fall's flame-colored leaves and trees, from a forest that blaze, often I find myself. I still would write. That an intruder from his purpose of terror be discouraged, I would write! Within the darkness and the chaos, amid the yells and screams and shouts and cries, some logic, some saneness to find, I would write. From the emergency-rationing of my thoughts I put, *A Season Interrupted,* together.

After The Rain evolved during a brief stay at a shelter for homeless persons in Hoboken, New Jersey. The shorter pieces of fiction, and remaining poems, were of the last five or six years, as I bounced around the Chelsea area in Manhattan. All were written in English. *Rhythm-a-ning,* is tribute to the art of, and to the people who create the music we call jazz. Though of late I've been regarding it as homage slightly more to pianist Thelonious Monk, who high-lighted the term, when he so-named one of his musical compositions; and to percussionist Max Roach, for whom I wrote, *Mop Mop*. From Archie Shepp we got, *Four for Trane;* Marion Brown gave us, *Three for Shepp*. The beacon of their music brightly glows this day still. My lifting humbly of voice, is but offering before the sacred flame, my own you might say, *For Max and Monk*. As I wrote *In The Night,* the voices I heard were Billie Holiday's and (mother of the murdered Emit Till) Mamie Till Mobley's. For me, irresistibly fascinating these women remain. They tasted of racism's bitter crop; yet in the heart even of a blighted forest defiant still stayed —

> *Let the world see what I see*
> *Let them hear what I hear*

For a voyage of discovery that would be forever *Outward Bound,* the music of a man called Eric Dolphy was fuel.

But with biographical info and other such sometimes irrelevant data, a writer should be careful not to burden his readers; he should, wherever possible, leave room instead, that his work would stand, mainly on merit. This I've always believed. As a result, I kept very little record, and find myself now often at a loss as to how I approached, or when I composed a particular piece. It was inspired by the British cellist Jacqueline du Pre, and at first, *Tum* (or *Tumkatum*) I had titled it — of the poem *You Jacqueline,* I remember; but not much more. Elsewhere, I am even less certain. My interest in Scandinavian mythology began, for example, when I was in my twenties. But a 2009 going into 2011 close relationship with a woman from Iceland who, more than acquainted with her country's legends, was not shy of retelling them; plus short stays (years earlier) in Denmark and Sweden, might both have encouraged, *A Station In Midgard*. Substance abuse, though long out of my life, on my memory still, had left its mark. I was not aware of it at the time, but as far back as 1991, I already had lost all contact with everyone who knew me in the past. When around 2013, I quite by accident ran into jazz-bassist extraordinaire, David Williams (whom I had not seen, God knows, for a period longer even than my incommunicado years), we almost didn't recognize each other. Through him, I learned that, among friends and family and foe alike, the belief was that I had died. Drug and alcohol-free by then, I decided to have fun with this, I came up with, *A Man Unheard from Long*. Whether we are young, or in years advanced, reside in a small town, or on a broad avenue in a sprawling city; regardless of our mood or social status, not many of us are immune to the quiet spasms the changing seasons sometimes bring. That would recall a near-forgotten escapade, mirage moments, the frenzied *haskara* and furnace fun of early-in-life summers, fiction I've wanted always to write. How many times a story I outlined, and had the work completed almost in my hands; but dissatisfied with the shape it assumed, as rough-draft allowed it to remain! Recently a friend realized an offspring. That, *The Ice-cream Van,* I would complete, seemed honor appropriate for the newly-arrived first-born—

> *Swift-chimed are bells*
> *In summer that early ring*
> *But wafts of brittle flavor*
> *Memory even when they last*

From years derelict with substance-abuse, the frequenting of nighttime hot-spots and after-hour clubs, with the dregs of society—pimps and prostitutes and dealers and addicts and murderers and thieves—as associates, dark whispers I sometimes in my mind hear still of, *A Kill In Harlem*.

A filmmaker supervising the production of a story he knows well, is familiar with the twists and turns of the plot, understands how the props were assembled, the way scenes are lit; hears the actors voices before they speak their lines, knows in advance where the villain lurks, how the heroine is saved; must of the final cut, have a point of view removed far from those a casual observer might share. On celluloid he put together the stimuli which, in a darkened theater, would shape the perception of others; his role now could only be analytical and non-subjective. This, I reasoned, must hold true also for writers of fiction and their crafted works. The case being such, like the cannibal reptile whose brood she must (lest she be tempted) abandon no sooner they are hatched, I wanted to not pay too much attention to my manuscript while it was being marketed. Writers who hover close to, and seem moved by, their own works, are being disingenuous, I thought. As publication neared, and I sat-in at conferences, met with people who were encouraging, did re-writes, poured over proof-reads, and whatnot, I started to look at things slightly differently, and got to a point where I no longer knew what I felt, or how I should react. The faded ink of documents long ago misplaced and forgotten, once more its part would play. An early girlfriend, delighted to learn I had not died, and that I was writing again, went out of her way to have delivered to me, a leather attache case (the first I ever owned; that I ages ago left it with her for safe-keeping, completely had slipped my mind). It contained papers still, photographs, and a few other things, mementos she over the years quietly had kept. Suddenly I had in my hands, material which predated not only the work I had done in Italy, but was looking at poems that were older perhaps, than just about any I had ever written. And though I did not at first understand why; I immediately recognized that, here were lines that would remain unsurpassed by whatever I might in the future even dream to achieve. Then I remembered! I remembered that the term, *Panstrum Denstrum,* used to be my juvenile cryptic own way of saying, 'All the things that were!' Written when I was a young man still, and reluctant perhaps to share them with others, the lines of that poem described of childhood friends: men of music, Allan Gervais, Earl Rodney, and Wilfred Woodley. Like myself, they were self-teaching of their craft; but unlike me, they went on, all three of them, to have illustrious careers. *Panstrum Denstrum,* honors them still.

> *The sounds random even*
> *With their instruments men create*
> *Sweeter than a kiss*
> *Sometimes will music make*

That words by myself written, would cause me one day with emotion to be overwhelmed, I never imagined. How wrong I was! How sadly wrong! How delightfully wrong!

E. C. Maxwell
New York, 2016

A Season Interrupted

It began not with a people, nor with a country, nor with a creed, or on distant corners, or in the mountainous regions of lands exotic and far; but closer; closer to home, within the forests of ourselves, behind the foliage our hearts. It began with the creatures that we are, and with a season that is ours—a season which though far from ended, one day still, will have run its course, and its cycle complete—

> *Fall's russets and reds*
> *Winter crystals erase*
> *To spring and summer*
> *They in turn give place*

We are like seasons. And when we are changed, and from the constricting folds and blinding shadows of our own selves moved, the crises and conflicts that plague us now, will cease. And the chaos that accompany them seemingly endlessly, will in oblivion—the oblivion of errant ideas—remain. A hand mightier than ours charts course. Within its incomprehensible ellipse, a sequence of months and years and centuries, determine our fortune and future, leaving us at times unable to fashion even our own dialog, or to venture a degree beyond the path

which is before us set. Our tranquil days into evening
turmoil sometimes erupt, and though we try to contain
them, through nights and in mornings further, continue
inexorably still to flare. Time—time's own tremolo—
will the door to this corrupting, convulsive period close.
The commonplace-now stand-offs and skirmishes and
protracted battles will cease, the disputes of war—and war
itself, with its legacy of bloodshed, its culture of subterfuge
and murder—even from the data-banks of our collective
memories, will one day be erased. In a world unlike the
one we knew, we'll discover ourselves, beings unlike the
ones we were (humans still, but *futurons* now), a species
changed, and from the outmoded implements of a bygone
age, forever turned.

> *But chortens we are*
> *To the copteron*
> *Though they overwhelm us*
> *We say still*
> *No*

No, we cannot laugh and applaud and cheer the fire
that come now from the sky. Nor can we with you at your
banquets feast—you celebrate the conflicts of the day!
For us the day is long, bitter and long; the sky above is
everywhere with venom filled. The cities drenched in flames
are not unlike the ones we call our own. In our dreams the
scorched and wounded there nightly loudly cry. And when
as if by lightning struck, we wake again, we are in our tracks
before them halted still, enmeshed in a curtain always of
tears. Except to herald a day disastrous as the ones which
preceded it, tomorrow—the tomorrow you promised—
never comes; never comes, but to edit a dream, or rather
an episode within a dream, an already-ended adventure,
begun again; begun only to end again, and to begin again,
as it always has, as it always will: with a discovery of

ourselves, with a discovery of each other, with a discovery of ourselves—again.

How memorable your voices are! How familiar, how compelling your cries, that from within a chorus of shrieks and yells and shouts, we heed them still! How like echoes quick we are at your sides, not at the same time distant, as in the mirage of a movie or dream, but from within an ensemble of wounded-eyes on a tapestry of battered images that are our own true replicas. How feigned the indifference in which like a fog we cloaked ourselves so long! How easily penetrable it always was! We too are bludgeoned now! Within the narrowest passages of this treacherous trail, we too are in the darkness beside you fallen! Question not our hearts, but know only that this burden, this grief, this sorrow, this melancholy journey is ours, *ours too*.

You are citing the death-toll! You are decrying the villainous acts!

You are saying,

> *What did we do*
> *What did we do*
> *We did not deserve this*
> *What did we do!*

You are saying,

> *These are our sons*
> *These are our sons*
> *Lest you forget*
> *These are our sons*

We will not forget! We will not forget! That every man is product of a sacred union, we will not forget. That he is the sum of his ancestry, and that he witnesses at times the sacrifice of his offspring, we will not forget. We will not forget death's master-toll. But forgive us if we weep for all the corpses that litter the blood-drenched battlefields of a conflict-scarred earth; among them of 'good kills', your own fair share, the sons of others. If for us, one kill is one to many, forgive us! If distant even in the far reaches of Kosmos, it is still too near, forgive us still! Give license to whomever you favor. Describe their exploits in the terms you imagine! Death by human hands often times is murder! And murder not only breeds murder—even at its best, it breeds only murder! If we regard it still 'a deed most foul', forgive us still!

We will not forget! We will not forget! The nature, the essence of the villainy, we will not forget. The names omitted, the cries unheeded, we will not forget. We are your fellow-creatures, we cannot forget. We ask only that you hear us. If only for a moment, hear us! But hear us still!

> *If the dead come now alive*
> *As once they were*
> *And yesterday's torment*
> *With them we again endure*
> *Together we would stride until*
> *We no longer share a common will*
> *If they remain tomorrow dead*
> *Than elsewhere more*
> *Beside them still we'll stay instead*
> *And the piper's drone and the solemn drum*
> *Will stem not limb nor grief*
> *But echo only more a long night restless sleep*

The faces of cherished ones—spouses, forbears, tiny offspring—appeared so vividly before our eyes, we reached-out almost to touch them, thinking this surely must be a dream, a savage dream from which we will at any moment awaken. But we did not awake. The blinding flash became more blinding, the intense heat so overwhelming, we no longer could determine whether we were experiencing after-shocks of the initial collisions, or whether subsequent smaller ones were occurring still; only that it thundered, all around us it thundered, even in our hearts; even in our hearts, it thundered so! Fear gripped us. Like a suffocating restraining garment, a deep cloud into which we spiraled, and from which it seemed, there would be no escape, fear gripped us all. The air was filled with cries. We cried-out the names of companions who moments before were shoulder to shoulder with us, and who, now in the confusion, clouds of dust and smoke, were vanished. Others cried-out, cried-out for their own companions, they cried-out again and again. And we cried-out again, but in response, like-cries only heard; the like cries of others; anguish cries, cries of the fallen, the lost, the doomed, the near-dead, the dying—

> *God cancel their mournful pleas*
> *That we would ourselves this peril flee!*

We tried to flee, but before we knew it, we too were felled, and found ourselves beside the gaping mouths and vacant stares, the motionless bodies and unfocused eyes. Some insane precocious deity had strewn them there like discarded broken mannequins, across an area it had decimated, and with which it played havoc still—

> *These were our dead!*

We looked upwards. We looked upwards and saw colossal plumes of smoke and orange, the tall structures engulfed, saw white-hot steel curled as ribbons in a summer wind. We watched with dread, *the sky!* This could not we thought be the silhouette of a man sailing through the air towards us, but it was! And there were others, and others still; other silhouettes, other men! One by one, from the stories up high they hurled themselves earthwards in desperate, maddening attempts to avoid the inferno which threatened to consume them. Some of us buried our faces in our hands and looked away. Others watched until not far from where they stood, bodies began landing on the hard concrete.

We malfunctioned. That day, just then, for a moment or so, for an eternity or so, we simply, malfunctioned. We lost our sense of color; and, having lost our sense of sound as well, found ourselves blindsided by silence: grim, grinding, gray, grave, and eerie *silence!*

Then—it happened! Like the disintegrating props and scenery in a monumental theatrical production gone wrong, the streets, the river and parks, familiar landmarks—our lives, our world—even the September air, seemed to dissolve around us. A door we thought would protect us forever had—while we slept—unhinged. Now reflected pale glimpses of our panicked faces, and the faces of others frightened as we, accompanied us, as alongside the plate-glass exteriors of buildings that were still intact we raced; and, like wounded ants, passed them, fleeing in the chaos of a nightmare. The Twin Towers had collapsed. Everything that was in them, all who were in them, had fallen to the ground . . .

Mayday! Mayday! Mayday! A near insurmountable barrier of sand and stone and gravel separates us now, stifling your appeals, impeding our efforts to console you. *Mayday! Mayday! Mayday!* We are tiny creatures trapped in an aquarium of stagnant water. You are distant out-of-focus and shrill. And though we are unable to distinguish them from our gasps for air and shrieks of horror and cries, your voices plague us still, and of your faces we are reminded. At arm's length again, you are with us again, you are smiling again, you are laughing again, we are together again; together as once we were in different times,

and on better days. You were less strident then. Ours were
amicable terms. Those days far though in light years gone,
remain closer yet, within our hearts and memories, locked.
In the depths of our despair, from upon even these rocks of
terror, we recall them still. And though we are lashed by the
tide of an angry sea, its raging turmoil obliterates all else
but your cries; your cries we hear of, *Mayday! Mayday!*
Mayday!
    You are sobbing uncontrollably. You are saying,

> *These are our companions*
> *These are our friends*
> *These are the friends of our companions*
> *These are the companions of our friends*

You are saying:

> *These are our country-men and siblings*
> *Our hearts and minds and limbs*

You are saying,

> *The authors of this tragedy in blood,*
> *should themselves be*
> *paid in blood, in their own blood, in*
> *their own life's blood—just as we with*
> *our lives, and with our blood, and*
> *with the lives and blood of relatives,*
> *comrades and offspring paid—*

You are saying,

> *They should find themselves alone—*
> *alone and adrift—on a sea of despair,*
> *and they should know that it was we*
> *who sent them there; sent them that they*
> *endure, as we did, the long slow hard*

*torturous journey which begins, which
begins always with leaden feet and with
sunken hearts, and which even after the
final sad farewells, never ends, never
ends*

You are saying,

*Their burden should be heavy too. Their
burden should be heavy. Though it be no
more than the ash of their comrades, it
should be heavy too—heavy as ours was
heavy, heavy as ours is heavy still—*

*These are our dead we carry
These are our dead!*

This is a building—the charred remains, the
smoldering shell of a building—in which we lived and
died!

You are saying,

These are our flags—at half staff!

You are saying,

These are our bells that toll!

In the silence, in the silence of the service, this
is the gentle rain that raps the windows of the church,
the same church in which it seems only yesterday that
wedding vows were being exchanged, and now, now this
bitter wind lashes hard the tear-filled faces of widows, of
widowed parents, of orphans!

You are saying,

> *These are the splayed fingers of my*
> *small son's hand, as he releases the dirt*
> *that falls onto the casket, his brother's*
> *casket, so deep, in the ground*

You are saying,

> *This is our cry*
> *This is our cry*

No, not even a syllable nor phoneme, nor nuance of your expression escapes us. For unlike the *outeron* (indifferent creature of an alien species), or the man-made *metalons* and drones that may one day a future earth survey, we are emotion and flesh. We are humans. We hear your curses before you utter them. We are humans. Your cries are our cries, too.

> *The grim dawn cancels not your grief*
> *Morning's gloom your faces wretched*
> *with pain obscure*
> *Nor shield even the torrent of your tears*
> *But our hearts make heavy*
> > *and our voices rasp-like too*

We hear your every word. We breathe even your sighs. Forgive us! Forgive us, if we are helpless before a persistent narrator, one who reviews our thoughts, supervises our actions, and solicits our comments. It is He who impels us to think! It is He who impels to act! It is He who impels us to speak! Forgive us now! Even as we speak, forgive us! But hear us—hear us still!

Worshipers of noise and fire
We heeded your imperatives
Did we not make way for your serried ranks
Who can dispute your right

But for a canon's glow
Not even the torrent you see
Nor all the corpses borne
Nor the veil of tears that is ours

We ask not the tally
Who their parents were
How they worshiped
                    from whence they came
Grief we only know is human

And that a companion betrays you
 Custodian of kill-power
Betrays you every day
Rampant death running still
                    its wanton ways

The dead are not comforted by cries of vengeance. In theirs that impenetrable realm, beyond time and temperature, beyond light itself and dark, colors are indistinguishable, one from the other, as are the flags themselves, nor are their positions on the staff discernible. Bells do not toll. In the abode that is death's eternal, silence—a vast silence—reigns. The dead themselves are simply dead. And do you think they care! Do you really think they care whether it was Orpheus, or the laws of physics, the rotation of the planet that caused the sun to rise—that the day dawned even, the day they were catapulted into a shock-corridor, realizing in a terrifying instant, that along with the showers of broken glass, the random objects, the shoe that contained a foot, their own limbs had before them flown like debris in the savage wind of a surreal hurricane! As, blinded by the lava of their melted eyes, they fell clutching their entrails, the burning shrapnel embedded in their flesh, do you think they wondered whether the morning's courier transported his lethal cargo, attached to a specially-constructed belt around his waist, on a hijacked airplane, by remote-controlled laser-guided missile, launched from an aircraft-carrier or submarine in an ocean close-by, or through light-years from another world! Whether he traversed the adjacent terrain, perched near a flag on the top of a tank, or rode out of hell on the wings of Lucifer himself, would not have mattered. The dead have but one cry,

Save us! Save us! Save us!

Now if after their bodies have been interred, their spirits confront us still, reminding us at every turn, that they perished, and that we survived—those souls departed long, those lives too soon cut short—could not their disdainful cries, angry curses, vile and obscene gestures be for all the world that lives intended, as well as for the assailants more directly responsible for their departure from it! Amid the humansplat, the waste-strewn rubble and smoldering ash, no doubt a charred-finger somewhere points; but at whom, for God's sake, at whom?

> *Varied and countless are its victims*
> *The reckless demon true*
> *Whose brood within us lurks*
> *Who walks among us too*

Even in its blood-choked rattle, even in death's whisper and gasp, you discern alliance. As each heart ceases to beat, it reaffirms (you say) the legitimacy of your cause. In the names of the deceased you campaign. Of the mass of flesh at your feet you say,

> *Your colleagues were guilty*
> *We made them pay*

Our dead have no names. We seek no ransom in their passing. That we are viewed with new and equitable eyes, allowed access to the middle ground of justice, is the only inheritance we claim. The mound of corpses, headless torsos, severed limbs, miscellaneous body parts—whose existence you one moment deny, and the very next, like trophies exhibit—are no more our colleagues than they are yours—though, sadly we must admit: they are no less.

You play the tapes! Even as they conspired you recorded them, vague portraits of men so similar in appearance, they might be members of a single family or clan, the 'irrefutable' evidence, splayed like a deck of cards in front of you. From where we sit shackled, we see blueprints, the lay-out of cities, parallel lines that are streets, the shapes of houses; larger rectangles representing schools, shopping-malls, hospitals, and other such structures; arrowheads superimposed over what might be densely populated areas; here and there, an X highlighted within a circle in the sky. We could not have taken those aerial photographs. We are earthbound creatures. We know only the faces before us, the faces beside us; faces that laugh when we laugh, and are moved to tears by even our sorrow. We could not have placed those symbols over your homes and cities, any more than we could have placed them over our own images in the mirror before us.

As to the names of relatives, even of childhood acquaintances, you seem informed. Sometimes you are hysterical, and demand specificity regarding incidents of which our knowledge is inadvertent, our memories clouded at best. One incident comes to mind. It happened long ago. It lasted forever. It was night. It was day. It was hell. We were on an expanse of water. We were shackled then too. Now we don't even know where our father is. Maybe he is still in Lagos—in Ikeja somewhere. Maybe he is up north in the circumpolar region where you had driven him. Maybe he died on the tundra. We don't know. We don't know! Why would you torment us! We don't know!

You are attended by a pair of hounds, their leashes firmly in your hands. But whether you are restraining, or by way of subtle messages urging, or keeping them primed, is not apparent. The one slightly ahead barks, growls. yelps, whines incessantly, but hardly bites; the other, whose bite is near-always fatal, makes hardly a sound, except for an occasional yawn, followed by a quick snapping of its jaws. Like conjoined triplets, your movements are deceptively fluid. Once you are upon your quarry, all is futile.

We admit! We might as well admit! That we are terrorists, we admit—the terrorists of terrorists; that we are saboteurs, the saboteurs of saboteurs—subversives of subversives, the spoilers even of the spoiled; we admit, rather than in a world amesmered and scared, at the convenience of others, complacent remain, to be branded so. We admit! We might as well, rather than allow you with your methods of new torture, to take us to death's threshold, stopping short always that we see its many faces (all congruent strangely with your own). We admit! We admit! We Admit! But let us all for once be honest! Even if we were indeed culpable, even if the signatures on documents you hold were undoubtedly our own; we agreed that they were obtained without coercion, without threats, or promises of any kind (not even the promise of a better tomorrow), the fact—the unchallengeable fact—that the countless millions murdered and tortured throughout the planet's history, met their fate by way of hands other than ours, still remains. The truth is, we lit no torch, we detonated not a single device—we didn't have to—save the ones that exploded in the hearts and minds of men, inflaming their desires, searing their sclerotic dreams with the fire of new thought, new ideals! Your edifices—institutions, monuments—born out of brains that atrophied, simply collapsed under the unsustainable weight of their flawed designs. If we are at all guilty, it is that we revealed the hallowed ground to be unstable; at worst, urinated into wells that were sacrosanct.

Did you not sniff the wind! The water had long been tainted; it corrupted all who came close. Had you abandoned your rigid posture, ventured once beyond the time-worn narrow path you so violently defended so long, yours might easily have been, might truly have been *giant steps;* the giant steps you so often, so proudly brag about. You might have saved us all. And more, far more than the discovery of Aleutia, America, and Antillia, new worlds with the blood of contingents old, red drenched; more, far more than if as you stepped onto the moon, you had discovered all, all there was to discover, beheld all the lights in the sea of stars that is Kosmos, you would have marveled still, marveled and rejoiced; rejoiced for being able with new and distant eyes a simple *blue-in-green* to view, the blue-in-green of earth, *new earth,* an earth that men would call (that men have always secretly, passionately called, *ama* 'mother') *ama-terra,* sacred solid ground upon which with equal footing we stood, a haven that was ours and theirs and yours and mine; the bonanza of a true big-valley, where crystal waters flowed.

No, we will not forget! We cannot forget! Memory is all we have left—memory and feeling. We will not forget. But is it not you who have forgotten, forgotten the most self-evident of truths, your fellow creatures, your mirror-images, your selves; forgotten Him—yes, even Him that is mafia, and all of Kosmos, *Oba;* the true *capo* who created you, who in His own likeness created us all, and whom as you have us stand now blindfolded and naked before you, you emulate; forgotten God! (You quibble now even of His name!) All names are His! He is the proprietor of names! There is no sound we utter that is not of Him, that does not describe Him, no sound; He is the keeper of sound, the maker of sound, the maker of the silence; yes, even of the silence, that is the absence of sound.

> *Barp ka nam*
> *Beta ka nam*
> *Nam ka nam*
> *Nam be nam*

Yet though He remains nameless and formless, through Him men–all men — are kin, and it profits not, the killing of kinsmen. Is it not you!

Is it not you who failed, who fails still to realize that politics polarizes people, that not only is there something rotten in the State, but that the State itself is rotting, and that the most state-like of States is ofttimes the most rotted of States; that more than anything, statecraft unsettles the tribes of earth, dissembles them (both chorten and grand) that they are, in a carrion-world, transformed into a race of carrion-men, at their own throats even! Is it not you!

All but your corner men and seconds, you forgot; the blitzkrieg of their media-craft and campaign, the daily image and analogy-mongering they practice, a scourge vile and worse than witchcraft that blights our eyes and clouds our judgment! Is it not you! In the all-encompassing mirror that is conscience, an elusive villain resides—find him! Your thoughts will be nourished. Look into the deceptive pools of ever-changing hues that are his eyes—the eyes of self—and know that it was self, it was you, you a long time ago who charted this course.

Wow, it was you who orchestrated the carnage. Out

of nothingness, you discovered yourselves like a beetle, gravity-bound, clinging to the surface of a planet that was paradise. You stood upright, and thinking creatures that you are, immediately foolishly dreamed of flight, dreamed of an existence above and beyond paradise. You created hell, the hell of your own nightmares—a hell that is everywhere, in an everywhere that is hell. Look! Look, Herr-Interrogator! Look into the eyes of hell! Begin! Begin again your probing! But this time to yourselves the accursed instruments attach, this time of yourselves the questions ask!

Amid the stench of burning flesh, the vile sickening odor of rotted decaying carcasses—ask! Among the grim-faced survivors, the weeping grieving relatives—ask! Ask the law-enforcers and rescue-workers; they are exhausted, numb; and after endless hours of gruesome detail, unable even to speak—ask them still! Ask the medical examiner, the emergency-room and mortuary attendants—*on both sides of the fence!* Ask them that most elusive and troublesome of earthly questions, ask them: Who?

Who on this shambles of a planet, in this might-is-right, wrong-and-strong, devil-take-the-hindmost order of the day; from within and against every ethnic group, for every reason under the sun, and with every device his brain could muster, commits these acts that so devastate us again and again and again? Who? You know who! You've always known! You may have to wrench your hidden heart of hearts, but have the courage this time to answer, to enunciate the words that in every language and culture, are the most difficult of all. Look squarely at yourself and say:

> *Dear God, it is I*
> *It is I, Dear God*
> *I maker of things, Dear God*
> *I destroyer of things, Dear God*
> *I, Dear God, I*
> *I, human*

After The Rain

Author's note: Little has changed. Ten at night the dormitory lights are off. At dawn, breakfast is just about ready; pastry and cake and fruit are available, sometimes all day. As shelter for people who are homeless, the church in Hoboken, New Jersey, to this day remains monumental. To the actual structure on Bloomfield Street, however, to the people who reside in it, the staff, past or present, and to incidents which may have occurred among them, resemblance here would be the effect merely of chance. Put together haphazardly these are at best random notes coming out of adventures of mind I underwent during a brief sojourn in that facility. By regarding them not too seriously—certainly not literally—the reader will do well.

Day remained bleak, and except for our own voices, soundless at times. The air weighed heavy. Night fell. The wind picked up. We quickened our strides. Debris whirled at our feet. We could not see the stars, and wondered whether clouds like the ones obscuring them would be with us still in the morning when we wake. It is afternoon now again. The temperature had fallen. By noon we were back to being seasonal. Under the weight of a downpour, the roofs rattled. The rain would stop. A drizzle followed. It would rain again. It would drizzle again, it would stop again. The sun shone hardly. Visibility stayed poor. It grew dark at times. The severity of weather that twenty-four hours ago appeared a certainty has not materialized. It is raining. Somewhere not far away it is raining still. Whenever it rains, or even when it is about to rain, especially at night, my shoulder would hurt.

The shutters banging loudly not so long ago, against the exposed or 'weather' side of the building across the street, are silent. Someone must have secured them. Except for a faint, every-so-often rattle of the windows within their frames, and an occasional break, in the otherwise continuous castanet-like chorus of the foliage rustling in the wind, all is quiet. The dormitory lights are off. I am standing not far from the window, looking-out onto the street. Staff is uncomfortable with this sort of thing. (Once it is past the hour of ten o'clock, they like us to be in our beds.) With the status of the weather, only I am concerned. The others are asleep, or resting on their blankets. It is drizzling lightly (than of the last hour's two or three sprinkles, perhaps a little less so). Cutting through the shaft of light coming from the street lamp outside, glistening needles of liquid at an angle descend, with droplets bouncing off the window, before becoming part of the quick rill falling from the ledge into what already must be a sizable puddle in the flower-beds below. A girl appears. As if from out of the night and rain, in the window's mirroring panes, a girl appears, her slender frame superimposed upon my own; the two of us together close in what seems a tender, though perhaps awkward embrace. She smiles. She smiles, and it is as if, the night itself—as if all of the night, is smiling. The night is smiling at me, to myself, I quietly say; but then, I think, no—no, it isn't! Night does not smile. No one is smiling. I am imagining these things. The needles of rain, the yellow light, the street lamp; the castanets and wind, are not real. The girl is not real. None of this is! The wooden stairwell creaks with the weight of one of the staff ascending to the upper floor. The stairwell at least is real, the rest I might have imagined. From beneath the closed door to the adjoining room, a faint fiery line of light escapes. That too no doubt is real. But there is no girl.

I am not standing at the window. I'm not looking at the rain. I am asleep. That's it! I am asleep, and cloaked in a blanket of dreams. If the rain should come, if the waters of a flood should rise, I'll be protected, protected in dreams, protected by that panoply of images that comes, that comes always, with night's cavalcade of dreams. Although night and dreams, I must not forget could both ways cut; both ways, yes, and like a young girl's smile frivolous in a moment, a hundred and eighty degrees, one hundred and eighty degrees sudden easy turn, I must not forget. The dread of night, I must not forget; the derelicts of night, on the streets of night. Under alcoves and awnings, within recessed areas of commercial buildings and other such structures they, where they find it, take refuge from the gusts of wind and sheets of spray. Now a deluge! A deluge is upon us now, flashes of lighting illuminating gray, a ribbon of faces, that with claps of thunder multiply; their anxious eyes with each moment more, made anxious more; each step a closer one, closer to an unimaginable doom, the beginning already to pour waters of a torrent, the unimpeded steady rise of an irrepressible flood. Rain and night. Night and rain. Still, the expected storm—the real rain that is—will not come, I don't think. At least it isn't raining now—well, not anymore, it isn't. Earlier-on, there was, I seem to recall (unless I was dreaming then too) not a tumult but a sprinkling; a sprinkling here and there, one or two, with gusting wind causing leaves to swirl, trees to dance, hanging signs on their hinges, back and forth to sway; the unsecured shutters on a building near-by to incessantly nosily bang. All is silent now, silent again; silent as night when I dream of night, often silent is. Although I imagine the rain must be somewhere falling, inaudibly lightly still.

Sometimes even after I wake, I hear, before I open my eyes, the faint droplets, and smell the sodden earth; I feel the drizzle cold and wet on my face. Full awake

I look beyond the window; and realizing that it is night still, drift slowly back to sleep; to dream; to dream again, of night again, and of the rain again. Day cancels my dreams; morning is with droplets on the window none, nor castanets crisp and early shrill, nor a flotilla September-browned of leaves with traces green-webbed of summer, spiraling above the fresh-washed asphalt; that propelled their air-borne excursion, no wind subsided, nor asterisk of miscellaneous shrubs disturbed, scattered close to the corner, near the curb, at the top of the hill; nor the hill itself; nor the sea beyond, with foam on the water, debris floundering with the tide. Maybe it did rain. There might even be, if observed purposefully carefully, evidence of an earlier down-pour: relict in the trash, an umbrella's broken metal ribs, protruding antennae out of yesterday's discards; tiny lakes, in the zigzag folds and hollows of an ensemble's despondent hills, black-plastic tilted near a narrow band of damp earth encircling a pool of water, the surface of which, the wind perhaps on the rise again, seems wont now to disturb again. On the air, a hint of moisture, a taste of salt awakens me! I see the sea! I see the waves breaking on the shore, plumes of spray, a juggler's toss of tiny dancing crystal spheres, rising into the air, for a moment motionless as if by photography frozen; curving, after a second or so, downwards again, before turning to spidery foam, along the shore. I am awake! I see the sea! Beyond the rocks at the foot of the hill, I see the sea! Visibility is heightened. I see the sea, I see the jewel — I see the sparkling blue jewel of the Tyrrhenian Sea.

The sun has not yet risen. Beside the curb, a man is standing, with a dog at the end of a leash in his hand. My first thoughts are that they would soon be gone; but the dog's continued interest in one of the dirt-filled grooves separating two squares of concrete sidewalk, provides reason (or a pretext) that the man interrupts his, to all appearances, leisurely stroll, while maintaining a standstill (though not without shifting his weight, I notice, several times from one foot to the other), the distance of a dozen or so steps, behind me to my right. This is my daily route. That I am here is no accident. I'm always here at this time of morning; rain or shine, I'm here. But as to our sensibly-attired visitor (shorts, T-shirt, sneakers) and his canine, I have a feeling that it is more than coincidence that positions the three of us, in the same city, on the same street, at the same time. Despite his apparent patience, and tender rapport with the beast, his air of domesticity not withstanding; the fact added even, that his gaze seems focused not in any one direction, but vaguely everywhere at the same time, our early-riser is, my instincts seem to be telling me, on an assignment of serious reconnaissance — one to which he has committed himself, with the fidelity, I have no doubt, of an epidemiologist reviewing an important slide, during the crisis hours of a plague. *Boungiorno! Boungiorno Signore!* He's a government agent; a member most probably of one of the newer, more savagely vicious, quietly lauded, so called 'elite' forces!

You think I would be fooled, eh! Come off it! Just come off it, man! At the same time — at the same time though, my own purpose of morning, my mere presence even, to a casual observer, to any observer for that matter, might not be so easily decoded. My idle air, general awkwardness, uncoordinated manner of dress; the fact that I'm not clean-shaved, nor hurrying off to work like everyone else, could be offsetting, I know — especially since it is at a glance obvious, that I am not one of the local townsfolk. To be truthful, it doesn't much matter where I am, my life-style and demeanor, in one way or another, runs contrary, it seems always, to those subscribed to by the people around me. For my present motionlessness, there is reason, though: the orchestra whose 'live' performance I'd been enjoying since I awoke and left the homeless shelter, I don't know, about twenty minutes, say near a half an hour ago, keeps getting disrupted when I continue to walk by a blast, it seems, of annoying static, inter-filtered with the opinions of an apparently inexhaustible radio-host, his campaign centered (if I'm getting it correctly) around a group of armed-forces personnel who, due to 'stress of combat', and because of some type of (collective, I suppose) brain condition, had killed a group of civilians (children allegedly among them) in another part of the world somewhere. They could not, because of *Military Law*—he argued—be held responsible for their actions in a civilian court. Moreover, he emphasized, to see it any other way, would be setting a dangerous precedent; one guaranteed to put a greater number of 'innocent lives' in peril. Of course, how the *innocence* of these lives (or the guilt, for that matter, of others) would be determined, he never disclosed. Such was the framework of his appeal. He was, I gathered too, without fondness for people he described as being, from shores 'other than our own.'

The expanse of blue-gray beyond the protective barrier (my elbows resting now on its horizontal top-rail, foot on the bottom, my right knee wedged between two of the verticals), is not the Tyrrhenian Sea. It is a river. Yes, a river. It is the Hudson River. And on second glance, the water is not blue; it is I would say, a sluggish this morning glaucous more than gray, at times even metallic brown. I'm not (though I often imagine that I am) in Italy. I'm not in Naples, I am not in Rome, nor am I on the coast of Sicily, on the plains of Catania, or anywhere close to the Tyrrhenian. Italy is far away. Let's visit facts. I am in Hoboken—Hoboken, New Jersey. This is the United States, the United States of America. That's Manhattan on the far side of the river. The behavior, moments ago, of the fellow on the hill, was not unusual. His was of no extraordinary scrutiny. His wife (or girlfriend) most probably had instructed him that the dog needed a crap. They enjoyed a pleasant night; he was happy, he complied.

He could not have been any less uncomfortable with our near-encounter than I was. He was not a member of any 'special force.' The poor animal (a French poodle, if you please) was not his partner or fellow agent; a dog it was, just a dog. And apart from a few here-and-there phrases I picked-up from watching Federico Fellini movies and spaghetti westerns, I don't speak Italian. What I said was, what I really said was, 'Good morning, sir!' And, not bothering to determine whether he had heard me or not, I glanced at my wrist, as though I were wearing a watch (my departing abruptly might, I at the time thought, be reason for suspicion); then, feigning as best I could, the body-language I hoped would give the impression that I was admonishing myself, I mouthed something like, 'Oh Shit—I'm late!' before quietly walking towards the river at the bottom of the hill.

'Morning Ladies!'

Advancing towards me, a couple of old girls are with brisk movement, covering the tree-lined walkway that skirts the river; I wish them a hearty one. They cheerfully respond, one of them lifting her hands overhead, playfully pretended that she would cartwheel—she waved and smiled instead. After a few steps, she waved again, and smiled again. Walking almost sideways now she manages, hesitating for a moment, one last joyful gesture (closing her eyes, tilting her head skywards, shaking it from side to side, as if to absorb all the morning had to offer), before joining strides again with her companion. *(My name is Rotschild Jarvis! I live in the shelter for the homeless here in Hoboken!)* I'm tempted to introduce myself, but realizing quickly how little sense this would make, I shrug my shoulders, and remain silent. The gestures and smiles were intended perhaps not just for me, but for everyone and no one in particular, anyway. I begin walking towards the

train-station in the opposite direction. I kick a few pebbles.
I hesitate for a moment. I spit at one of the trees. I call out a
name—anyone's name, someone's name! Maybe it wasn't
a name. Maybe I just made a sound. I'm beginning to tire.
I should rest. I'll think of Silvia. Yes, I'll think of Silvia,
and I'll rest for a while.

Methodically, diligently, I begin removing the damp
debris from a bench upon which it had been my intention
peacefully to repose; without reason, I change my mind.
I'm at another bench now, one rattling loudly as I use
my foot to remove the damp leaves that covered the seat.
Why I chose this method, I am unable to say. Maybe I
am trying to determine its sturdiness as well. Whatever the
reason, I'm causing enough of a disturbance (apparently)
to attract the attention of several passersby (one or two
of which made sure that I saw the glances of disapproval
they threw in my direction). I know what they're thinking.
There ought to be a law! Alright then, there ought to be
a law! So what! Perhaps there would be a law regarding
every single thing on the face of this Godforsaken planet
of ours one day! Perhaps the fact that the unkempt,
disheveled and somewhat bloated man of indeterminate
age, whose grime-covered sneakers rested neatly side by
side on the ground beneath his grime-covered feet while
he comfortably slept on the adjoining bench, should just
then chose to fart several times—and quite audibly each
time, too—did not help matters any. Well, sorry! Sorry one
and all! But what do you want of me! Tell me please, what
you want me to say! Be thankful he isn't rotting, is what
I say! In parts of this world of ours, even as we breathe
now, the corpses, when they are not being devoured by
dogs, are decomposing in the streets—or didn't we know!
We didn't? Well, that's life, I guess! And since 'shabby'
and 'unsatisfactory' (our radio-host believes), are the ways
we treat our boys in uniform, that's war, too (I think); a
different kind of war, but war nonetheless. A man on a

bench may be veteran, he may not be. He may be casualty. Maybe he's not. Call it what you like. Call it modern sorcery. Call it the statistics of the day. Call it the best or worst of times, I don't know. Tell you the truth, apart from my headset failing me (always, it would seem, at the most inopportune of moments), I really don't care. I don't give a rat's behind about anything or anybody. I have my own fish to fry. I've been engaged in one protracted private war or another for God knows how long (all my life, I guess). My shoulder is beginning to act-up again. I get exhausted quickly. With each passing day, I'm forgetful more. And as if all this isn't enough to fill my plate, I'm beginning again, to think often again, of Silvia again.

Maybe I'm getting the shit all wrong. Maybe I'm getting it twisted (it wouldn't be the first time). I'm being too hard on myself. I'm being too hard on everyone. Maybe. These people are not concerned as to whether I'm on my way to work or not. The problems of shelter residents (or 'inmates', as I prefer to call them), wouldn't interest any of the locals, so long as we don't make unbearable nuisances of ourselves. From the looks of things, these people are pretty well laid-back. They have, most of them, achieved what they've wanted out of life (money, property, an uncomplicated existence), or so it seems; they don't much care, I suppose, about anything else, be it civilian deaths in some remote country on the other side of the globe, or a new resident at the local shelter, being not quite sure, as to how precisely, or on which bench, he wants to settle his restless (and, as far as they are concerned, God alone knows how unsavory) behind, in the briskness of an autumn morning. They don't know who I am, nor care even that I exist. Sometimes I am not sure myself, not so sure of myself, that I am myself; even that I'm sitting now on this bench, I'm not so sure! Anyway, people around here probably never even heard of a place called Viareggio, let alone the silly nonsensical stuff I allowed myself to be part of over there. Viareggio is far away, far away in Italy; and, who knows, the way my brain functions lately, my exploits there (like so much that plague me these days) might turn-out to be imaginary, anyway. There are no French poodles on Hoboken's municipal payroll. Trained sea-gulls aren't circling overhead with electronic surveillance equipment attached to their undersides. No one is following me. Nobody is on the roof of a Manhattan warehouse, lying flat on his stomach, using cameras with powerful state-of-the-art telephoto lenses capturing my image. There's no need for me to walk always in the shadows, or to wash my hands every five minutes, or to meticulously wipe my prints off of everything I touch. No one is after my DNA. There are no microphones in the flower-beds; no secret holding areas (no camps) being prepared in Montana and Alaska, no government plan to eradicate the homeless, or to purge society of its handicaps, the insane and other less that useful individuals—no secret underground factories mass-producing near-perfect human-like robots to replace them. I shouldn't worry. This isn't Nazi Germany. The coffee at the local fast-foot restaurant isn't spiked.

Of course, it's the medication that's causing me to think this way; I know that! I should never have undergone the therapy; the social worker kept insisting, but I should never have agreed. The medication makes me this way. The shelter is 'down with it' as they say in the streets. Of course, they're down with it! Look around you! Everybody's down with it. Everybody is down with the program—everybody! What do you expect! You think you're entitled to, that you would receive decent medical attention—for free? Come on! Give us a break! You think you're not paying for room and board—that we are, all of us, these days not paying a price even for the air we breathe! Hey! Status counts. This is America. It may not be Nazi Germany. But this is America, my friend. Status counts. In America status always will count. These are experimental drugs, can't you tell! Unauthorized drug-testing is, for today's alchemists, a well-traveled, lucrative high-way. The big drug companies call the shots. The authorities, particularly at the upper levels of government, are hand-in-glove with them. A lot of money is being passed around. Have you ever taken a good look at the shelter's honcho-in-charge, Dr. Zimmerman — Dr. (Heinrich?) Zimmerman! How much longer you think it would be before he retires to Montana with a ranch the size of a small city, and an army of servants and attendants! As far as I'm concerned, *Herr-Commandant* would be a more than appropriate way of addressing him. In the brochures he is described as an eminent psychologist. He's an arrogant fool. I don't even think he is Jewish. Matter of fact, it won't surprise me if, a group of Nazi-hunters and their supporters appeared outside his office with a dossier of damning evidence, one of these days. After all, what better place for unauthorized (and undoubtedly dangerous) experiments than amid society's unfortunates! Where better than in an unsuspecting New Jersey town!

Rotschild Jarvis: guinea pig. Uh — Oh! Now isn't that's a good one! I must remind myself to be thankful for the not-to-be-taken-with-alcohol warnings labeling my medication. Good Lord, had I not read them, the result could have been catastrophic! I might have reached into the black plastic trash-bag in which I keep my belongings. In the section reserved for fine spirits, I might have discovered a previously over-looked bottle of Italian brandy. I might have knocked-off two or more good stiff ones — at yesterday's luncheon, or perhaps with last evening's brisket-of-beef dinner! God, a drunken bum is a drunken bum, no amount of warnings on the labeled-vials containing his medication, will transform him into anything but; nor deter him from his purpose of the moment, or alter his course of destructive action, once — having had that first swallow — he is risen out of the starting-blocks, so to speak, and embarked on his mission of high-speed mayhem! I don't like this medication. I don't need it. I have a good mind to throw it in the river—or better still, throw it in Dr. Zimmerman's face when I get back to the shelter this evening. Director-in-charge—a dickhead! A Goddamn dickhead, that's what he is! I don't like this medication. It makes me drowsy. It makes me drowsy and it makes me sleep. These days all I seem to do is sleep. I sleep in the shelter. I sleep in the waiting-room at the train-station. I sleep on the benches overlooking the river. Waiting for the sun to rise, I sleep. I sleep—I sleep and I dream. Sometimes I dream I'm far away. Sometimes I am far away. Sometimes I am far away in Italy. Sometimes I'm looking up at the clouds sailing pass the Tower at Pisa. Sometimes it's autumn. Sometimes it's summer. Sometimes the sea is cold. Sometimes as I walk along the beach, the stones are cold. Silvia was cold. The last time I touched her she was cold. Even when we kissed in front of the fire, even with the Vechia Romana brandy, sometimes even after we made love, there'd be goose-bumps on Silvia's arm. Sometimes I think Silvia and I are stubborn leaves, in the cadence of a changing season, clinging of summer's branches; of its diminishing glow and fading colors, despondent; unable to say good-bye to an ended-already escapade, to disentangle ourselves from a too-long suffocating embrace that would leave one of us pale, that would leave one of us pale and . . . I don't trust the staff at the shelter. I don't trust any of them. I don't trust that freaking Dr. Zimmerman, or whatever his name is. I sleep when I'm waiting in his office, too.

He's seen me! Wouldn't you know it! Great Britain, I think he's from. He stays at the shelter off and on. He's going to want a cigarette. Of course he is going to want a cigarette—he always does! Avoid his eyes! Shrug your shoulders! Be nonchalant. *(I'm sorry I don't! I don't have a cigarette! Sorry! Sorry!)* He'll contemplate saying something else, but would walk away. I'm sure he does that only to annoy me. Why can't he manage his addiction to nicotine! *Sorry!* Why can't he exist without bothering others! If he really needed something, I'm sure he'd know precisely where and how to get it. The British accent is key, apparently, to the many doors welcoming always of him. People are impressed. Maybe I should trill my Rs every so often. It's beginning to warm-up. I wish he would stop bothering me. I'll sit here for awhile. I'll sit on this bench. There's a breeze. Let's sit on this bench. Let's just sit right here and enjoy the breeze. Wouldn't it be nice if everyone everywhere trilled their Rs, trilled their Rs and spoke with British accents, and sat on benches smoking cigarettes paid for by other people, while waiting for the sun to rise! Sure. That would be nice. It would be . . .

But for a handful of crystal pinpoints visible still beyond the fibrous hues of salmon and purple and lilac and blue, the stars have surrendered the sky. Shadows that with morning's light not yet full, danced silent and gray, their earthly corners too abandon. In quiet spasms people are caught. Railings and monuments and trees vibrate. With strides that are near-tremors, an ever-plodding messenger is affirming once more, the frontiers of his reign. Above a serrated skyline, beyond the rooftops and antennae and pylons and cranes; the tall columns and advertising billboards, a bludgeoning ballooning fiery disc of power, rages; rages new, rages again, rages orange and huge and blinding and scalloped; illuminating all, diminishing all, conquering all. An aircraft's vapor-trail is gold-crested. The summits of high-rise buildings and other tall structures, amber-bright gleam. But for an exaggerated feathered boa, flanked here and there, by wisps of gilded clouds and stretching, it would seem, from horizon to horizon, the sky above Manhattan is clear. There's a breeze. The river is calm, a trio of ducks rising and falling with the undulating water. A barge is being hauled upstream. Someone on deck is walking towards the stern. A pair of shorts, a T-shirt, sunburned arms and legs, interrupt my gaze; a man with a huge mustache and irregular gait, followed by a boy on a bicycle with a dog running at his side. There's hardly a breeze. A girl in her late-twenties, her sports apparel doing justice to her more-than-well-developed frame, walks by. Silvia had a body like that. It is getting warmer. Silvia's hips were wide. A flag flies red. A flag on its staff flies red. The sun clears the skyline. From a little to my left over on the Manhattan side, a snake's tongue of reflected golden radiance darts across the river, igniting its surface with a fiery band of near-blinding sparkle. I close my eyes. I imagine the water lapping against the stones. My headset is working. My headset is working again. The flautist trills, sustains a note in the lower register, cuts it, holds it— holds it long; and, as if suddenly somehow, he too were by the spectacle of the morning thralled, interrupts his breath, allowing his cadenza of cascading arpeggios, an unruly rest. The orchestra swells. The audience explodes. Something is happening on stage. The sun disappears. Everything turns red, the water, the leaves on the bench beside me, everything; everything is red; red as blood is red, red, red again. During one of the intermittent breaks in the now near continuous muffled applause, someone coughs, clears his throat. Someone gasps. Someone is gasping for air. I am in Nuremberg. I am in Nuremberg, Germany. Someone is gasping for his life. The trial begins. The applause dies. The chorus of sobs and cries and shrieks and wails and moans, subsides. Dr. Zimmerman's chair is empty. The Chief-Prosecutor is addressing the court.

I appeal to your consciences! I appeal to your consciences, gentlemen! These men are responsible for the most heinous crimes in history. I appeal to your consciences! I appeal to your consciences! These men . . .

A cello soars. A seagull cries and flies away The Chief-Prosecutor continues his address. The flautist trills. I close my eyes. Everything turns red. The sun warms my face. Everything is red again, the spheres of liquid, the plumes of spray, the wisps of clouds, the sky above them, red, red again . . .

I

It was late. But Silvia and I stayed. We always stayed. Even when it was dark, and the lamps on shore were lit, and the stars shone above them in the sky, we remained. That night the buildings were velvet shadows. There were other boats on the water. I could hear voices. I could hear laughter. How could they not hear me! It was as though they were far away, far away as everything now is far way, the stars, the sky, the girls playing volley-ball, the cyclists in their oranges and greens and gold; the boys on the soccer team, far away. Silvia is far away, submerged beneath the rubble of a house of cards that collapsed; trapped amid a miscellany of cascading debris, shredded documents, and turned-over bales of straw. We ran from city to city, and from town to town, avoiding her parents. A summer, the fragmented mementos of a summer by the sea, a sea whose unpredictable surf and swells reflected the stars, separates us now.

The wind picked-up. The surface of the water rose and fell, rocking us one way then another, again and again. Suddenly we were borne by what seemed a thousand misshaped pyramids and domes, from which sheets of shining spray rose upwards and lashed against the side of the boat, fragmenting each time into a myriad of misshapen lozenges, and droplets, and cones. How could they not hear me! I cried for help. Silvia was hurt. I held my breath. I held my breath as long as I could. Under the water. I could see her. I could see Silvia's flailing arms. I should have stayed. I should have stayed with Silvia. I made a mistake! I try to tell people, I made a mistake! Nobody listens when

I tell them it was all a mistake! I can't stand it when nobody listens! I cant stand it! I can't stand people who don't buy their own cigarettes! I don't like people who make guinea-pigs out of others! The butchers of World War II! I hate them all! The tympani and bass-clarinet confront each other. The waves are battering the boat, lifting it up and tossing it around! I am unconscious. Yes, I am unconscious now. When I awake I would remember the black depths, I would remember the night, the night and the stars dancing in my head; that there was debris on the water, I would remember; I would remember too, the salt and the foam, and the sea; yes, I would remember the sea, I would remember the dark and the sea, that the sea, the sea itself was dark; that it was dark, and that it had sparkled, that it had sparkled, I would remember. . .

Entry: Sometimes a granule of substance, a stubborn flavor from half-way around the world, an unexplained—an unexplainable—bitter-sweetness, lingers; and, as if freed suddenly after being restricted long, dances defiantly elusively, on the pallet of the memory, evoking the feeling again, the warmth again, of a long-gone, yet still not-ended escapade; of stones moist and cold thousands of miles away; an amphitheater seen from the window of a pensione in an obscure village, a piccolo borgo by the sea; a string-quartet rehearsing in the piazza; the timbre once again of a woman's voice, as half-asleep she responds to a man kissing her gently on the nape of her neck, kissing her and whispering, Silvia! Silvia! Silvia!

Among the accused, in Nuremberg at trial I am, shackled and seated in a cell. No-one spoke on my behalf. The packed gallery that applauded each sentencing, now cheered voluminously unceasingly that mine should be the death penalty as well; that I too for my crimes must pay, they demanded. Yet of the derisive shouts and whistles and jeers, one voice fragile and faint, held me, it seemed, in disfavor than the others less; one voice, 'I'm sorry,' said; and even as the others fell silent, continued, 'I'm sorry,' still to say. Gasp-like finally, it drew breath, and in person, before me stood. I must have sleep-walked, for I was no longer on the bench, but standing now directly behind her, gently but firmly, holding on to her left upper-arm with my right hand, attempting to pivot her towards me; attempting it would seem, to put into motion, choreography that would result in the two of us sharing a kiss or, in our being at least embraced: the young girl with the shapely legs she was (the one who looked like Silvia). It was her voice, that wakened me from the depths of my dream! 'I'm not Silvia,' she said, 'I'm sorry! I'm not Silvia!' I released my grip. Taking time to enunciate each syllable, she several times repeated the words, 'I am not Silvia!' I wanted to tell her, I wanted to tell her that I too was sorry, that mistakenly I thought she was someone else (though I wondered myself whether this was entirely true). I wanted to say, I'm sorry. But my throat was dry, and as much as I tried, found myself unable to speak. Somewhere deep inside, I must have with some dark logic reasoned that, the sound of my voice, even by way of an apology, would be more egregious than my having laid hands on a young girl who was a total stranger, in a public place. That was a close call. Under different circumstances, even with the scenario modified, I could have found myself in the hands of the doggas. I was still not yet fully awake. Ingesting deep of the morning, left me on feet that were unsteady. When I exhaled, it was as if from upon the stairs of a dark tower, the uppermost treads inexplicably I had scaled, and there now remain unsure of my footing; unsure of the walls beside me, that they would crumble; unsure of myself, unsure of what waited below. I don't like slippery slopes. I don't like brushes with the law. Someone could have called the doggas. Even under the

most benign of circumstances, I dislike having to countenance of individuals who by their apparel and manner
advertise that they are privileged of coercive power. I am
Rotschild—Rotschild Jarvis. None of this should be taking place. Mindful more, I should have been—mindful
more! The old Rotschild would never have read from so
untidy a script.

A few nights ago, something peculiar occurred. I
didn't know what to make of it then and there. But since
the encounter with the girl on the walkway, the episode
keeps replaying itself in my mind. It was close to the shelter's 10 P.M. curfew. I was headed in for the night. I was
a little anxious. My shoe-laces became undone. In attend
of them, I stopped (quite by chance) in front of one of
those stores that sold provocative female under-apparel.
My shoulder had been bothering me, I rested it against
the window. Inside, an ensemble of about five or six female mannequins formed part of a display in progress.
One of them was dressed with a pair of frilly white-lace-
trimmed, mauve and black panties, fallen half-way down
her thighs. In one hand she held a long black-leather whip,
part coiled over her shoulder and under her armpit; in the
other, she must have carried a dagger, for one rested now
ornate, shiny, and made of what look like bronze on the
floor beside her. All this, though somewhat out-of-the-or-
dinary, was in itself not alarming; a prankster, or perhaps
careless window-dresser, could have caused those items
to be placed as they were. But then, I noticed something
else—something which resulted in my being extremely
disturbed. A little further inside the not fully-lit store,
among the random boxes and strewn fabric, someone was
crouched in an unusual manner. He must have realized
that I had become aware of his presence; no sooner our
eyes met, than he quickly pretended that, he too, was concerned with his shoes. And this is where things took on
a curious flavor. He and I were almost identically-attired

and, as far as I could tell, of near the same weight and height. I stood up, so did he. And when not wanting to give the impression that I felt in anyway threatened, I casually continued on my way, he quickly, I could see from the corner of my eye, exited stage left; and, mimicking near every nuance of my movements, began to morph out of himself, with the near-by wall giving him way, so that, as one would through a vapor pass, he entered it, was briefly non-visible, before emerging, seconds later, walking in-synch and parallel with me still, inside the darkened abandoned kitchen of the Chinese restaurant next door. What this meant, whether it was in any way significant, I'm not sure. But it started me thinking. People have been acting strangely. Quite often, especially when I journey at nights, I would become aware of movement and footsteps, whispered instructions, the rasp of metal, as in the adjusting of a saber within its sheath, a muffled cough, or some such sound, coming from a group of individuals, obviously following behind me close. I would change pace. I would remain motionless for a while. I would make a sudden turn. Still, as if my pursuers and I were by some unalterable command forever-linked, their footsteps remained near-echoes of my own; even when I hurried, even when I stumbled because of some irregularity in the sidewalk. Yet the few times I had the courage to turn around, no one would be there — or I would be confronted by something as innocuous as a pizza-boy managing his deliveries, once even a somewhat startled (obviously recently-wed) couple fussing over a baby in the carriage they were steering. Whatever the case, I am convinced that my movements are too predictable. And though it may not be necessary (not yet perhaps) for me to go so far as to alter my physical appearance (as I had done with theatrical make-up, once or twice in the past), I should at least vary the routes by which I approach and depart from the shelter. I ought to be careful. Strange things have been happening. This is not the first time. This is not the second time. I'm walking long. My mind is far. Incoherent suddenly of thought I become, unable to determine my purpose of the moment. With the cobbles beneath my feet uneven, the ground suddenly would shift, causing me to unruly dance. A silent haze is mine. I into blackness fall; to awake only after an eternity (it later always seemed) in a city, I remember benign and friendly well, hostile now and threatening, its familiar streets and promenades into darkened alleyways turned; the facades of buildings but walls of welded bricks unadorned with doors or windows or relief of any kind, except here and there dark enclosures from which eyes, hidden and furtive, determining my measure peered. (Later, smocked-attendants would secure my limbs and torso, while the gloved-hands of shielded figures inserted wires into an opening at the base of my skull.) This feeling that I'm being targeted, could be imaginary (a dream perhaps, nothing more), my brain attempting to heal itself. The brain has that capacity they say. On the other hand, a diagnosis however painstakingly arrived at, is that of a fool when one and the same (as well don't they say) is he, the physician and patient, who partakes of it—or is it, with himself for a client, or a client for himself that a lawyer is, or isn't, sometimes/always, *whenever,* usually can . . . be? I don't know! It doesn't matter! I'm not thinking straight. I'm not thinking straight, right now. The last days, in the little town, the sleepy little town on the water's edge, I can't think of its name—a fishing village it was, a row of quiet houses with bluish walls, flowered gardens, and gabled roofs that sloped down to the water's edge, on a tiny island in the Adriatic, the same things happened, the very same things . . .

There are puddles in some areas; in others, no more than a few damp patches. The sun has gotten brighter. The temperature, already high, might reach—I don't know, maybe higher than it was yesterday. There was something about the young girl, something about her demeanor, her eyes. For someone whose morning stroll had been interrupted in such an unusual manner, she maintained remarkably composed. She should have been terrified. Maybe she was terrified. Maybe remembering Viareggio, she was terrified. Maybe she was acting. She wasn't acting. This girl was never in Viareggio! She was never in Viareggio, and she isn't Silvia! *(Come-off it!)* She could have remembered nothing! There was nothing to remember, in the first place! In Viareggio nothing happened. In Viareggio nothing ever happens. The failure of an insignificant voyager to make himself available to the authorities, concerning a minor incident of which he was as much in the dark as they were; his at times ostentatious behavior, and surreptitious departure, blown out of proportion (as was all else that happened back then) made for good column in the small-town tabloids, that's all. The girl may have had Sylvia's eyes, but she damn sure wasn't Silvia! She really didn't even look like Silvia. She simply came out of the image-mold (by fashion-houses of Italy years ago manufactured), that remains trendy today still among young females. She no more looked like Silvia than a thousand other Silvia wannabes look like Silvia. She happened—she simply happened to be enjoying her early-morning walk in the sunlight, that's all. There must have been good reason still, for her composure, her being so without emotion (her more ghost-like than human appearance). She had been programed! That's it! That's what it was! She was programmed. Yes. Like most law-abides within the crowded cauldrons of today's crime-riddled communities, she read from a defense manual (the *wunder-hund* that is media made sure of that) how a situation such as the one I inadvertently brought into being a moment ago, should be managed. Trust no stranger. Check! Distance yourself from the poor and the homeless. Click! When within earshot of the aforementioned, pretend to sympathize with their problems. Don't ruffle feathers! Yes. Yes. Be polite! Stay calm! Trust no stranger! If there is but a hint of anything out of the ordinary—even if there isn't— sound the alarm! Alert the authorities!

She should have reappeared by now. Traveling in the opposite direction, as several times in the last forty-five or so minutes, along with the others, she had done before. She should have reappeared. It's been twenty minutes! It's been longer than that! She seemed relaxed. Perhaps she only seemed relax. Just before she went beyond the curve at the end of the walkway, her strides quickened; she (memory serving me correctly), then fired a couple of quick glances backwards in my direction (in the manner almost of some- one checking to see whether the coast was clear). It's been half an hour—it's been more than half an hour. She's on her way home. She tired early. She completed her walk, and did what she would every morning at this point nor- mally do: she exited the walkway (by yourself unnoticed), and headed home. This is not a normal morning—nothing about it has been! I'd seen her before. I always notice her. The last leg of her walk is usually towards the train station. She would, when she was headed home, cross my field-of- vision always from left to right, never from right to left! I've watched her. From this very bench, I've watched her. I've watched her more than once. She was scared. I saw it. I saw it in her eyes. Her eyes were distant. They were the same as Sylvia's eyes. I remember Sylvia's eyes. They were the same. They were the same as Silvia's eyes when . . . Something—something is wrong! She's in full flight! People are beginning to realize that something is wrong! She frantic brushes pass the morning joggers! Something is wrong. Look! Look! Near-exhausted, she collapses pale and limp, onto the shoulders of a passer-by (whose befud- dlement, as he tries to make sense of her terror-filled eyes and incomprehensible gestures, agitates her further). In fits and spurts, she tries to tell him something, but could only flail her arms and gasp and cry. Heads turn, eyes widen, faces in disbelief and horror, contort! A crowd gathers. The poor child's life would never be the same! A walk along the river-front would never be the same! She needs to be sedated. Filth! My daughter school is not far from here—do something! Someone must have seen him! The assailant might still be lurking around! He might be lurking around somewhere! *Kallakaap!* The crowd turns vociferous. *Sambady kallakaap!* She managed to escape! One of the straps on her halter-top is broken! She's lucky to be alive! She managed to escape! Her arm is bruised! Look! Look at her arm! There are scratches and welts on her arms! The death penalty is too good—too good for that sonofabitch! KALL A KAAP, *WILL YA!*

A female Sergeant stands guard. A paramedic is in attend. Trembling with fear in the back of an ambulance (a huge blanket or shawl around her shoulders), the frail child seems no more than fourteen or fifteen and—white? White! Hold-up! I remember olive-skin—olive skin, well-formed limbs; twenties, perhaps thirty, nice thighs, a decent behind! This girl is skinny as a rake! Could so dramatic a contrast the result of my imagination be! I mean, I know I have my memory moments but, not this time; not this time, I don't think! What's gong on! What's going on? Elementary! Elementary is what's going on, friend! Elementary! This girl, in the media (and later in the courts), could for a convincing performance, be depended upon more reliably now—is what's going on! This due, of course, to the not so surprising fact, that she is (let me guess, let me guess now) herself no longer, but a hungry-for-the-lines-fed-her instead, brazen actress wannabe unknown with whom the authorities, not wasting time, had skillfully replaced her! Such chameleon-types are not unheard of, and not hard to find nowadays. . . while, numerous lately are the instances in which a witness' shy reticence causes a guilty culprit to be freed; the use of a competent (as victim) surrogate, not only insures punishment, but spares the actual victim additional trauma as, naturally, would come, with a trial and all that it entails. Alright! Alright. My mistakenly accosting one of the local females, a harmless in itself incident, yes, could, let's take a guess again here, be impromptu turned, into one which, under suitable circumstance, would be God-sent and golden in terms of rewards for enforcers of the law, the politically ambitious, and other watchdog type activists groups and individuals who, believing (perhaps honestly, perhaps not at all), that their communities are under siege, see nothing wrong with 'tidying-up' the loose ends, routinely 'altering' the unruly aspects of criminal allegations. That by their so doing, fact might be into fiction—fiction just as easily into fact—turned; with 'evidence' being little more than cosmetic, the regurgitated scenarios of half-forgotten movie folklore most of the time, hardly anyone concerns himself! This fill-in-the-blanks approach resulting often in the *pret-a-porter* one-size-fits-all railroading of hapless individuals, in-custody brutality, counterfeit trials, and sham displays of 'justice in action', happens, simply happens, to be the order of the day, that's all! At the same time, should the strategy of 'victim replacement' and doctoring of evidence not hold firm, questions at trial arose, as to who actually had been assaulted; whether a second girl, her replicated-image already indelibly embossed in the minds of an ever-frightened public ('eye-witnesses' among them, let's say) had been at the location, had been at all present on the waterfront walkway the morning in question, at the time of the incident, prosecutors and law-men, the townsfolk solidly behind them, need only admit, need only explain (begging the court's pardon, of course) that, perhaps because of 'honest mistakes, yes', there could, there could have been—no, we cannot (your Honor) rule-out the possibility, nor at the same time say for certain, that 'unfortunate discrepancies' may not have 'crept into the skeletal details' of what otherwise would have been ('and still is, we believe') solid honest evidence, and so on, and so on; overlooking not the fact 'far more relevant', that we are not yet 'out of the woods' as to just how many young victims this 'serial molester', beg the court's pardon, 'serial molester', may have traumatized; investigators overwhelmed (everyone believing) had only begun to uncover, and at this point, could only imagine the nature of the atrocities the *serial molester serial molester serial molester serial molester serial MOLEST-er* might have had upon the young minds he visited. Full and accurate account, difficult always in these types of cases, may never be determined, and so on, and so on, and so on. Their admission (regardless of the nature and extent of impropriety involved) would result, needless to say, in but an adjustment of torsion (little else), a tightening of the screws, so to speak; plus, of course, all around voltage increases at the electronic device by then secured no doubt painfully already long at the scrotum of the accused.

Off stage in the wings, so to speak, ready to take their places among the rapidly gathering (and, naturally, already well-ignited) crowd, an ensemble of furtive eyes ebb and bob in a swirling mist above the asphalt surface of stagnant lake. Muffled and faint, as if laboring out of a deep hollow or cave, a terse chorus of siren-like voices frighteningly audibly continue to rise; piercing now, and with each passing second, cold and shrill and angry more: a legion of psychologists, psychiatrists, forensic experts, DNA analysts; religious personages, psychics, psychos, local-politicians, priests, racist nuts, fanatics, activists, and a host of other individuals, local and national citizens of conscience, voraciously chomping at the bit, jostling each other, as they await their cue to spring into action—depending, of course, on the result of a (compulsory, in these cases) medical examination, for which the girl, let me see now, probably at this very moment, is being prepared no doubt to undergo.

In the wan interior of a building teeming with activity not far, always not far, from the center of things, the men for whom, in the maintenance of order and law, *seek and collar* is of purpose always utmost, informed of the threatened welfare of one of their city-folk, react as they've been programed—as they've programmed themselves—to react: they shelve paper-work, suspend their interrogations of dangerous felons; and, abandoning their posts, begin to make ready for, what many of them already secretly believe, would be a 'more than routine' engagement, falling over themselves almost, as they reach for automatic weapons, bullet-proof vests, stun-guns, restraints, canisters of mace, concussion grenades, and the like. Nerves are on edge. His half-eaten doughnut fallen to the floor, a burly veteran with an expression stern as steel, in slow-motion grimaces, reaches for his hand-gun, takes aim, squeezes off a few make-believe rounds in the direction of the wanted-posters on the bulletin board in front of him. At no one in particular he, shifting in his seat, half-smiles and winks, while lifting the weapon to his lips, and blowing away imaginary smoke rising from its nozzle. Choppers are taking to the sky. Traffic is re-routed. Sections of the city are cordoned-off. I WANT THAT BASTARD OFF THE STREETS! I WANT HIM OFF THE STREETS!

Having concluded his briefing, the 'big-guy' exits, his larger-than-life-size silhouette gliding across a map of the region so enormous, it occupies almost an entire wall. In the muffled sustained thunder of a battalion on the move, the heavy feet of men weighed down with weaponry and equipment, trample across the stone-courtyard in back of the building. With canines straining at their leashes, they climb into an assortment of utility vehicles. Their weapons are loaded. The canines are hungry. The men—most of them, of ruddy complexion, in good health, fine spirits, and excellent voices, their vengeful battle-cry several times raise: *Viareggio! Viareggio! Viareggio!*

At the crosswalk, the morning commuters advance, but not before several of them, towards one of the benches that line the sidewalk, scowled and inquiring, their gazes near in tandem direct. The figure half-reclined upon it, is livened. He stretches, dusts himself, dead pans, wears a silly grin, stretches some more; then, as if interrupted by a void or chasm, is frozen almost, behind a vacant stare. In a ritual not unlike the one which preceded them, the presently-halted group will soon partake; the same heads will turn, the same eyes will narrow, the same minds will question. As the lights again begin to change, the figure on the bench suddenly realizes, that he must regard each and every one of these disparate bands, with scrutiny.

Of their dreams surfing no doubt still a river, with which they are accustomed, they notice, not any of them, color nor detail nor twist and turn; whirlpools and eddies, nor rock nor islets, nor miscellaneous debris, that might temper the urgency of their early rising; but see of themselves reflections only, unfolding on the broad canvas that is space and time. Discarded candy-wrappers, the gum that sticks to their shoe, spittle on the ground, cigarette butts, soda cans, styrofoam containers, anonymous strangers; the shifting sands, the broken bricks and displaced gravel of their journey, will have escaped them. From their corridors of cobweb and darkness, reliable witnesses out of this crew gliding near-silent by hardly would emerge. A scenario as predictable as, and (except for calender) near-indistinguishable from the ones that preceded it; a cycle of images and events, replayed on the makeshift stage that is morning, will for them suffice: the sanitation crews that came and went, vendors enacting their rituals, a store-keep adjusting displays in his window, a greengrocer surveying pyramids of fruit; rush-hour madness: coats and hats, pocket-books and scarves, backpacks and brief-cases; umbrellas, wisps of smoke, the smell of fuel; people, a conveyer-belt of people being swallowed by the huge canister that is the train-station at the other end of town; television's early shows, coffee, coffee and cakes on the tables in the shelter still. (An innocuous overture, a kiss that failed, is all that would have been observed anyway!) Out of a dozen or so young men at the water's edge, two closer to the pier than the others, from the pack, with flourish depart, their brief flight ending not far away. Halted now, they are staring at something above them in the air. The accosting of a young female shouldn't and (unless non-mistakenly part of a larger scenario), isn't likely, in these times of lawlessness and chaos, to cause concern, wide-scale or otherwise. At the same time, with the memory of similar incidents juxtaposed, the encounter with the girl might seem innocent and of moments fresh, when it in fact may have occurred (if at all) long before the present time, day, or, even when. . . whereas—O.K! O. K-a-y! O.K! Let's assume, let us assume that imagination all this is—better still, let us assume that it isn't—that if not of the present morning, certainly coming out of the confusion of the last two or three preceding ones, on the walkway, an egregious offense (or one perceived generally to be so) was committed; behind every mask-like countenance and frenzied stride that passes now, a feeling of outrage simmers, a show-down (if we're not within our wits) but moments away, the situation more volatile perhaps than on the surface appears. The doggas? No! These men aren't the doggas. They're not part of an undercover unit! We find them (or a similar group) at the very spot, weather permitting, close to the pier, almost every single day, limbering exercises, eye and body coordination, their of the moment focus; a soccer-ball just-bounced, the wearer of a light-colored sweat-shirt and three-quarter length pirate-pants (buoyed by the cheers and shouts of encouragement from his colleagues) propels it upwards again. Guys. Soccer guys—of all but themselves unaware! Johnny Dog, they're not! The nucleus of a quick-formed posse? Come on! Guns, badges, handcuffs, and the like, they clearly do not possess.

At the shelter, the tables are empty, the cakes and coffee consumed, of their daytime escapades, the residents are already in pursuit. In this neck of the woods, at least in this neck of the woods, all is. . . well? All is well—all is well. Be mindful still! Morning though most of the time without witness or record, could of great discomfort a bearer without warning sometimes be; propelling tired consciences beyond their accustomed periphery to dwell and focus! The quick gesture of a changing traffic-signal or vehicle's blaring horn jolts them sometimes, as if out of an agonizing dream, back into real time, real life, real fear. Suddenly, like dead fish on the surface of a poisoned lake, the full bloom screeching tires of day arrives: accidents, robberies, attempted abductions; news bulletin, failed kisses, handshakes, politics, murder, traffic congestion, a torso surfacing; a torso being recovered from the bay, murder, a torso, murder-suicide, rape. . .

Traffic this time of day unless interrupted by official activity (fire, a water-main break, an accident, and the like) usually with a frenzy moves. Now for some reason, the line of cars and buses and trucks, is almost at a standstill. From an SUV, a man wearing a suit, and carrying a leather attache case alights onto the sidewalk, near the middle of the block. Nodding apologetically as, here and there, interrupted strides permit him leeway, he crosses the stream of pedestrians (their faces reflecting the urgency of the hour, and their need to reach their destinations on time). His polished shoes, motionless now before the paneled-door of a nearby building, the suit hesitates, looks around, before inserting a key into the lock. The door opens. Once inside the River Realtor's tiny street-level office, he immediately begins talking on the telephone, gazing as he does so, across the street, at the corner near the bank, where a young man is handing-out free newspapers, and advising passers-by to,

Have a nice day! One block away on the opposite corner, a contingent lock of colored bright-orange hair is, at the same time, by the wind aided in its attempts to distance itself from the scalp of a somewhat portly, close to middle-aged woman, who offering a near-toothless smile, every so often adjusts the dome of her head-gear, that she might accommodate the unruly strands. Hawking what must be a rival paper, she too, of passers-by asks that they, *Have a nice day!*

Somebody missed his appointment with his parole officer. Somebody's other brother mother sister-in-law has had a baby. Shah don't go with that girl no more. He live in Brooklyn now. On a bench in the sunlight I listen and I wait and I watch. It is warmer, already warmer than the forecasters had predicted. Last night in one of the neighboring towns, not far from here, there was a shoot-out between the doggas and a pair of carjackers—close to the block on which the other brother mother (?) sister-in-law (?) lives. It was on television. One carjacker was killed, one was wounded. The baby was premature. No mention of a young girl being assaulted. No chopper in the sky. No mention of a young girl being assaulted could be good. It might be bad. The doggas could be tricky as hell when they want to be. Tricky as hell! Don't fall asleep! Don't sleep! Don't. . .sleep . . .

By the time I realize that a patrol-car had arrived, its occupants (both male, and both in uniform) had already crossed over from the far side of the street where they were parked; and were bearing down on me fast. A run for it? Out of the question—they're too close! I could shoot my way out! But I doubt seriously that a hero sandwich in one hand, and last night's banana in the other, would match the fire-power these guys carry. Before I know it, they're on top of me! I'm expecting the customary request for ID. They passed by as if I wasn't there! Eventually they turn into the entrance of a huge building nearby. Without realizing it, I had been sitting almost directly in front of the municipal building that is City Hall. The uniforms were on their way to work. Before they entered, one of them looked directly at me and, narrowing his gaze, shrugged his shoulders in a condescending manner, as if to say: 'Hey! Cheer up, guy!' His intuition had told him that I was harmless—and helpless! He had important things to do, criminals to put away. Even if something did indeed seem not quite right about my person, it still would not have been worth his while, not even worth the paper-work, I guess.

Hey! HEY! Don't stand there in front of me looking stupid! Go on about your business! You hear me! Just go on about your freaking business! O.K? Punch your clock! Kiss your bosses behind! Do whatever it is you do everyday. Sit on his genitals! Just don't look in my direction! I don't like people staring at me. I don't give a shit! Hear me! Right now I just don't give a shit!

How did I get this way! How did I get so goddamn insignificant and non-threatening, so almost invisible; without my reservoir of personal power, unable to muster (even the appearance of) the brute-force, the sheer brute-force, that count for so much in today's world! God, even the trash-cans seem challenging. I could overturn every last one of these stinking trash-cans! With a sledgehammer, I should demolish the benches! Uproot the goddamn trees! Hurl a brick at the mannequins in the windows! Let's see what that fool in the shadows will do! Yea! Let's see what he'll do when I hurl a brick in the window! Mimicking me! Go mimic your mama, fool! That's what you should do! The girl no more looked like Silvia than any other girl who sometimes looks like Silvia looks like Silvia! So she wasn't Silvia! So what! That doesn't mean I'm crazy. It doesn't matter! Nothing matters. I'll run-in to Silvia again. We lost contact with each other, that's all! I'm Rotschild!

I'm Rotschild Jarvis, I say! I'm the one who pulled Silvia out of the bay! Silvia wouldn't be 'presumed dead' right now if it wasn't for me! I saved her! I saved her life. I'm no joke fella! More than once! More than once, I was suspect in criminal cases! My picture appeared in newspapers and on television! I was a criminal once—a wanted, dangerous criminal! You hear me! You hear me! I was! I was! And I'll tell you something right now, right now—yes you, you with your self-satisfied Tuesday-follows-Monday, Wednesday-follows-Tuesday, walk-the-dog in-the-morning, well-ordered, clean underwear every day, no-nonsense, stupid little life! I could tell you a thing or two! I could tell you about the years on the run, the years in Italy, the years in France; the nights in Vienna and Amsterdam! I made fools of the best criminal brains in Europe. I kept more than a banana and a tuna-on-a-roll in my pocket in those days! I drove a car. I lived in an apartment. I carried a gun—not a fake gun or starter's pistol on any thing like that, a real gun! A real gun! I had a girl. Silvia was my girl. I was, I mean I am—I mean, I . . . can't remember what I mean! Why can't I remember! Shit! Why can't I remember even my own name sometimes—I remember! I remember! Yea, I remember! I remember! Some of it! Some of it, yes! Yes! I remember some of it! I remember still! Not all of it! Not all of it! No, not all of it! But some of it, yes! Some of it, sometimes! Sometimes! No! Yes! Rotschild! Rotschild! Rotschild Jarvis is my name. Yes, Rotschild. . .

Life's sudden squalls play sometimes cruel havoc with us all, as survivors of fallen flights we, for reasons one or the other, seek refuge from the turmoil of our personal storms, so many individuals from so many avenues of life, compressed often into the taut stratum of a single season, crammed together all in the same space at the same time: a prison, a shelter for the homeless, a summer-resort. Out of boredom, perhaps because of some primordial desire to appear important in the eyes of others, we spin our tales; and get caught often in the harsh web, the unforgiving nanse, of our own fantasies. The storm ends. We disperse. Separate in time we go. But the sun eradicating all traces of the rain, forces us to make use, of its defining light, to on our lonely pathways behind us and around us look; to see ourselves (if only briefly) for the pathetic creatures we sometimes are. Truth descends like a scabbard, and leaves us often reeling, confused and afraid. The truth, the real truth, is: I hardly knew Silvia—I never got the chance! She was one of those girls, one of those rich young girls, enjoying a summer by the sea. I happened along. We made love twice—I think! Not quite two weeks later she already had moved on. She exited my life just as unexpectedly and unceremoniously, as she had entered it. I wasn't even in Italy when she died, and didn't learn about the boating accident until months later. But we had (with a group of others) not long before taken a photograph together. It nearly is night, the temperature mild. In a cardigan-and-sweater set, her hair windswept, a black-pearl necklace, with matching earrings, Silvia is a dream. Slightly to her right, I am pressed close behind her, my left arm encircling her shoulders; my right, bent at the elbow, raised skyward (the hand slightly abducted, the index and third finger splayed into a V for victory sign) over my head. There are clouds above us, a hint perhaps of moisture in the air. We are wearing smiles. That photograph appeared in one or two European journals and magazines, with the caption more than once: *Silvia and friends.* When, the following winter, I found myself shivering, penniless, and frequenting the coffee-houses of Paris, for the benefit of whoever would listen, I simply invented my own versions of the events surrounding her death. It was an accident. The girl never intended to kill herself! It was an accident, I tell you! We were to be married. I was on the boat with her the night she fell. She failed to surface! She must have struck her head. I dove under again and again. Exhausted and near death myself, I had to be dragged out of the water. Some people thought that, in a jealous rage, I had murdered her. Others, knowing how much we loved each other, feared that I might 'do something' to myself. She died an agonizing death. She went peacefully in my arms. We intended only to fake her death, in order to get away from her parents (who disapproved of our relationship). Something went wrong! She's not dead. I telephoned her last night. She's not dead. She's not dead, I tell you! My every move is being watched. No one knows I'm here. I am being followed night and day. Rotschild Jarvis is not my real name. Silvia's at a secret location. When it's safe, I'll join her there. Rotschild Jarvis is my real name, but I don't use it anymore. I'm not he! We're not having a conversation. The words you're reading now are not about me, the incidents they describe never took place. The photograph was doctored—as were all the documents relating to the things that happened that summer! You never met me! You never met *him!* When we took the photograph, I was second from the left, not extreme right, as appeared in some of the magazines! A type-o/switch-o? Walls have ears. A movie deal (in which I might play myself) is in the offing. Silvia might be carrying my child . . .

For a while that kind of babble, stories like those (and others), bought me hot-drinks and cheese sandwiches. But like the photographs, and newspaper clippings I forever carried, like my own pathetic life and deteriorating memory, they soon became rumpled and stale. Now I get confused, unable most of the time to distinguish fact from fiction; unable, it would seem, to get arrested even in front of City Hall in a quiet New Jersey town. God, that business with Silvia was nearly thirty-five years ago! Thirty-five years ago! Imagine that! The majority of people on this street weren't even born when all this was taking place! Nobody's interested. Nobody's interested in the senseless ravings of a delusional old man, who refuses to take his medication, and who, in the mismanaged street-theater of his tormented existence, often forgets even the lines of his own fictitious biography, while he night and day wrestles with the gorgons from the past. These people have their own lives, their own unadulterated summers to enjoy. Here every girl on every street is Silvia, she's her own Silvia; and she is beautiful, even as Silvia was beautiful. This is their town, their New Jersey town—not Italy, not Paris or London or anywhere else in the world, but Hoboken; Hoboken, New Jersey (Hoboken-on-the-Hudson, or whatever else they choose to call it). They are its main attractions, its headliners, the home-team; they star not in fading memories, nor in the revivals or remnants of a dream, but in the three-dimensional, live-in-color glint and sparkle, the mica and granite, of their own now-moments. God, it is I who am the menacing misfit, the out-of-place unfamiliar persistent annoying ghost, always present, always watching; my own existence, unexplained, uncelebrated, and unpleasant. I, Rotschild Jarvis, am the oddball, not the bloke with an English accent, nor the figure with grimy feet huddled on a bench in the park; nor the panhandler, nor the hawker of morning papers, nor anyone else. Having spent the night on the basement floor of a church on Bloomfield Street, this morning like an uncontrolled *jagnaat,* I too-early stirred, the kid beside me making noises as he slept (though it was I, some say, who talked even when I was wake, to myself; and that, debris they would towards me often hurl as I loudly nightly snored). Me! *Me!* What a laugh! Rotschild Jarvis, the experiment gone-wrong; the voyeur, the face outside the window, the face on the other side of life's window, looking in, always looking in . . .

II

It is evening. The sky is overcast. The undersides of clouds are, as if with the glow of roman candles lit. There must be a festival somewhere. The glass in my hands, like the liquid inside it, is warm. There's hardly a need to swallow. This brandy whets the appetite. Inhale! It dissolves in the mouth, it evaporates like the first-time kiss of first-time love with a beautiful woman; a beautiful woman who, silent now, for a while is silent still; then in ecstasy blossoms; moments later, near silent again, half-cries, half-whispers, of you begs, Don't stop! Don't stop! More! More!

Girls are rolling-by in cars, and honking their horns. There is a festival somewhere. People are crisscrossing each others paths in every direction. There's something about the sound of a woman's heels as she hits the sidewalk. There is something about feminine laughter, something about the smell, the very smell of a woman. This unexpected bonus, the sudden return of summer temperatures, is creating contagious mayhem. The orchestra is in the theater. There are crowds in the piazzas. Shelter be damned! The air-waves are static-free. Dr. Zimmerman be damned! Maybe this evening all over the world is beautiful and warm. They are dancing in the streets of Nuremberg, Germany. Maybe it is still 1936. Nanking nights are yet undisturbed. They are torching the camps in Manchuria, destroying evidence of unspeakable atrocities.

War criminals are being secretly pardoned, guaranteed immunity from prosecution for their crimes, I don't know. I don't care. My headset works. The flautist is playing. It is night again, our night again, our night; night at the opera again! In its orbit already of orchestrated unpredictability, a vintage rolling-ever-onward craft is nearing full speed; to be part of this turbulence, to be hither and thither tossed, not caring, not knowing what comes next, is the very purpose of this venture, the joy of it all! An eternity separates us now from familiar territory we will in the future revisit. Street-signs and store-fronts, the facades of buildings, our regularly dependable marker-points, receding now blurred and distant, will return solid again, staid again, intact again. They'll welcome us, as along private paths, we trundle back into the refuge realness and focus of our week-day lives, the morning Monday, the afternoon Monday, Monday-night! But—not yet! Between then and now, an inescapable *haskara* reigns! I'm in the Mile Square bar on Washington Street, Hoboken's Main Drag. I know the lads. They know me. They know who I am. If I should fall short, they'll let me put a little something on the tab. *Yes!*

Aaaaaaaah, yes! Y-y-yes! Thenkyor! Thenkyor! What! Uh! No. Boy were those weather forecasters wrong! I said: BOY, WERE THOSE FORCASTERS wrong! They don't know what they're talking about most of the time. You can't believe half the things they say! That's . . . that's good! No, I don't think so. Absolutely? Absolutely? Ah can't—not for certain—say! Bob! Hey Bob! Pardon me! BOB! Yes! Yes. No! Yes. Not at all! Over here! Over here, Bob! No. Over here! Oh shit! You know something— I tell a lie! You're right! You're Ab-So-Lute-Ly *right!* The ferry runs from . . . the ferry runs from Brindisi in Italy to the Island of Corfu, *not* to the mainland, not to Greece itself, not to the mainland—to the mainland, no! I stand corrected! You were right. You were—excuse me! Wait a minute—right! Excuse me, sir! They *theorized*—they only theorized that her cellphone had gotten away from her; and that, in attempting to retrieve it, she banged her head and fell into the water. That was only a theory! A theory, sir! Yes, sir! Yes! One of many, yes! No one knows for sure what happened. Of course, it was big news! Of course, it was big news! *Europe is Saddened,* I remember, one of the headlines read. No! They never recovered a body! Who said that they did! Who? What? You—you don't believe that, do you! YES, we talking about the same incident: the daughter of the Italian industrialist! Trust me, I know exactly who you mean! In the documentary—I don't care! I don't care! I don't care! I don't care what was said in the documentary! Listen! Listen my friend! Let me put it this way: You could drag the Mediterranean, the Tyhrrenian, or whichever sea you want to, one way or the other, from now until the end of time and back again, you'll find not a trace of Silvia Bertolini! Why? Why! For the most fundamental of reasons, sir! You'll not find her, because she's not there! Simple as that! Listen to me! Listen to me! Listen to me carefully! Silvia is not dead! Yes, she fell overboard. Yes, she hasn't been seen in public since—but she didn't die, she survived! How do I know! How do I know? Now! Well, now! That's a good question! I'm the one who pulled her out of the bay! How's that grab you! You're talking to him! Yes. Yes. I am he, yes. Yes, my name is Rotschild Jarvis. Yes. Yes. Yes. You never heard of me! Of course you've never heard of me! You've never heard of me, because I had the good sense—shall we say, I've always had the good sense—to keep what used to be known of in the old days as a 'low profile', that's why! That's why you never heard of me! That's why. Anyway, the facts—the real facts—of that story, and the part I played in it, were never disclosed to the media. In these type cases, certain details coming out of the 'big picture' are kept always (and with good reason most of the time, I might add) away from the eyes and ears of the general public. Anyway (God rest her soul) I made sure she survived. That's the main thing. Nothing else mattered. Finding myself in the midst of so terrible a circumstance. I did that which, I'm sure you would have done; that which any decent-minded human-being—the man next door, the man in the street, anyone—would have done, if he were similarly placed. I didn't even have to think about it. God, it happened so quickly! Going into the water, she took a blow to the head. She took a nasty blow! I couldn't do a thing to help! At that point, no one could, except for the man upstairs. He chose, as is his way sometimes, to not intervene. We have a saying in Italian—you don't speak Italian, do you? I sometimes find it easier to express myself in that language than I do in English. We have a saying in Italian, *Uomini propone, Dio disporre!* Roughly translated? Roughly translated . . . roughly translated, it means: 'It's up to the man upstairs!' She sustained, through their lawyers her parents claimed, 'damage to the head and torso.' In my attempting to rescue her I suffered myself lacerations of the shoulder; the scars hardly noticeable now, I experience every so often still, excruciating pain, especially when it rains, especially when it rains at night . . . She was named after her grandmother, you know, a second or third cousin, I'm not sure which, to the then Countess of Alba. Her full name is: Alexandria Tatiana Francesca d'Alba, Silviana Bertolini. The incident was hush-hushed, of course. As to what precisely they could and could not reveal, the international media were given instructions, which surprisingly (perhaps not so surprisingly) they followed to the letter. Her parents couldn't bear the embarrassment of a severely handicapped daughter. They warehoused her. They stuck her away (I strongly believe in Switzerland somewhere), then told the world that she had died. God how could anyone be so heartless! We're talking flesh and blood here! I know the truth! Though a lot took place while I was sedated, barely conscious, and being transferred from one location to the next, I know the truth. I hope that the doctor who signed the death-certificate sleeps well at night. We—we secretly were engaged, had planned even a wedding at sea! I would. . .have married her. . .even. . .if—MONEY DIDN'T HAVE A GODDAMN THING TO do with it! Who said that? Who mentioned money? Who are you, sir? No! No! No! No! No! Seriously! We were never introduced, were we? You couldn't help, you couldn't—ah, you couldn't help *overhearing!* No shit! Well, try and not miss any of this! Listen carefully, my good fellow! Bizarre as it might seem, I was under the impression that my friend here and I, were having a *private* conversation. And I can't—not at any juncture—seem to recall either of us bidding you a welcome to join. Do us a favor! Do us a favor, eh! Get out-a here! Just get to hell out-a here! Go on! You goddamn pervert! GET OUTA HERE! The nerve! The absolute nerve! What? You're very kind, sir! Thenks! Once again, indebted I am to you! Where was I! Excuse me for a moment, will you! Excuse me! Will you please, sir! Land-lord! Landlord! Would you put it in a proper brandy-shak-er this time! That should do! That's . . . that's fine! Taar! Everyone wants to believe that Silvia is dead. No Prob-lem. I know better. But even if that were the case—even if that were the case, won't you agree that I should . . . have been . . . informed, as to at least where she is buried . . . as to, as to . . . EXCUSE ME! Wait a minute! You're not talk-ing to *me,* are you madam? DON'T tell me to lower my voice! No! No, don't tell me to calm down, either! It's Saturday night! This is a bar! People get loaded! This is what people do in a bar! They drink! They drink, and they get loud sometimes. And I didn't bother your girlfriend—if that's what she is, and if that's what you are wanting to imply. She initiated our brief conversation while you were doing whatever you were doing for such a long time in the ladies room! All I asked of her was whether she could spare a cigarette—Oh shit! Oh shit! For that sort of thing, they nail you to the cross around here, don't they still! I'm sorry! I'm terribly sorry! By some inexplicable lapse of memory, I might have forgotten! I'm sorry! I'm sorry eh! *(Today's sex-toys would understandingly be more rewarding than the awkward abrasives of yesteryear! Take advantage! Take advantage of them, Madam! But leave me to FACK alone, would you please! Nice bed of snakes you're wearing, though!)* Where was I? Yes! Yes. Silvia. Silvia parents! Her parents never thanked me, not even a word! You know what I think! I think they would have preferred she had rotted at the bottom of the Tyrrhenian, is what I think. Perhaps they resented me for having saved her life, I don't know. I don't know what to think anymore. At the same time, no one could convince me that their gangster associates were not behind everything that happened to me since then, least of which were the rumors— and I mean vicious rumors—which began to circulate, some persisting to this day, in this very town, would you believe, about me still. I was this, I was that, I was the other! I was strung-out on drugs. I was dealing drugs. Come on! Suddenly I couldn't get a hotel room anywhere. Everyone demanded money up-front for everything I wanted to purchase. I was—it was whispered—connected with a secret priesthood, involving, God of all the stupid things you could imagine, 'bestial, cannibalistic, incestuous necrophilia!' Now, tell me, what does that mean! What the hell on earth does that mean! The lines apparently were word for word lifted from one of the promo posters for an Albanian horror-flick *(Droplets of Blood,* I think it was called), that had, I was told, a decent run in local movie-theaters, the summer before. Anyway, their strategy worked. They muddied my name! They ruined the business I started! They caused me to have to leave Europe. Still, as I've time and time again made it clear, I hold no malice towards anyone! The gossip-mongers had their tabloids to sell. I have nothing against them either. To fully appreciate the things I'm saying, you must bear in mind though—you must bear in mind, that for awhile I was riding pretty high. A brash young foreigner, out of the blue arrives, starts his own business, drives an expensive automobile, struts around like he owns the town, his constant companion, a beautiful daughter-of-the-land, local celebrity—not exactly the formula for winning hearts in rural Europe, is it! At one point, the services of a private investigative agency was brought into play. I could be in some way linked (they reasoned) to a number of women whose disappearance coincided (claimed they) with my arrival and, years earlier, brief presence in a (nameless for now, we'll leave it) little town on the Adriatic. What came out of their inquiry? Nothing, of course! Nothing at all! The women, except for the ones that didn't exist in the first place, were all located alive and well, and (judging from the photographs in the local newspapers), distanced, wherever they were, not too far from their daily helpings of pasta, one or two of them. The *carabinieri* (that's what they call the doggas in Italy) hounded me. They left messages. They staked-out places I was 'known to frequent.' What they really wanted to do was charge me with murder. I caught wind of the plot (someone inside the Bertolini household by telephone had alerted me); I slipped out of the country before they could make their move. Anyway, they couldn't charge me with murder! To do so, they would first have to prove that Silvia was dead, and they couldn't do that, not without producing a body, could they? They—could? No, they couldn't! I don't think so—I don't think they could! Anyway, I wasn't taking chances. I hot-wired a car, and took-off in the middle of the night. Things got rough and tumble for a while (going as I did most of the time by way of a not-too-often-used little-known Roman route that was perhaps as old—I found out the hard way—as Tiberius himself). It took several hours before I crossed the border into Austria. Once there, I was taken in by locals, who (learning of all I had gone through) risked their own safety to make sure that I was comfortable. I hope someday to repay them. Things like that you don't forget easily. Silvia's father, Fabbio, is an extremely powerful and (as I discovered later) vengeful man, with his own skeletons in the closet. It was rumored that he had had his brother murdered (so that he could marry Silvia's mom, and inherit the family holdings). Now you see why I may never feel safe. Hey, this world of ours could be a very small place when it wants to be! With his kind of money, you never know! Speaking of money! Landlord! Landlord! How much do I owe you, sir? How much! Didn't my friend pay for the last round? Yes. Yes. He and I were having a discussion not more than a minute ago! Y-y-yes! He was wearing a suit and tie. He—he didn't? He didn't pay for the drink, that's what you saying. O.K! O.K! Well! No! You misunderstand me! That's not what I meant at all! I'm simply saying that my belief—my personal belief, that is—is that he wouldn't have under normal circumstances done anything like that. It may have, at the time, slipped his mind, that's all. That's all I'm saying. No, I don't remember his name. Alright! Since you want to make it an issue: it was Bob! Yes, I think it was Bob. It was Bob—though I fail to see why that's relevant here and now. He didn't pay for one drink! Put it on the tab! I'll take care of it, I said! Where's the problem! It was . . . it was more than one, more than one drink you say! Look! O.K! I'll take care of it! You know me! You've seen me before, haven't you! I'm Rotschild Jarvis. Everyone knows me! The regular manager—what about the regular manager? The regular manager is not in tonight. O—Kay! Hey! Hey now! Hold-up a minute now! I mean! Let's not get carried away! Believe me, I understand your position! I understand full well how you feel—how constricted the little enclosure allotted you in this your corner of the planet must be! I too have, in the past upon occasions more than once, discovered myself beholden and subordinate to others. The last thing I would expect of you—the very last thing, believe me—is that you would have to breech the no doubt stringent pathway determined by your employers and higher-ups. But try now to understand me. Let's try and understand each other here! Let's just give a listen to what I am saying. I need a drink! Damn it, man! I need a drink! *I CAN'T EVEN GET A GODDAMN CIGARETTE! I LIVE RIGHT HERE IN HOBOKEN FOR GOD"S SAKE! I CAN'T GET A CIGARETTE!* I—I should what? I should 'buy my own!' Clever! That's really clever! *UP YOURS, MADAM—AND WITH A RUBBER HOSE IF IT FITS!* How about that! How about that, eh! *HEY! HEY! HEY!* Bartender! I'm talking to you, man! I'm talking to you bartender! Just give me a drink, will you! You have Italian brandy! You have a glass! Pour some of it into a glass! Hand it to me! You can do that, can't you! Can't you! You can't eh! You can't! You're a dickhead! A GODDAMN DICKHEAD! You heard me! You heard what I said! You're a—you're a Goddamn dickhead! Yes! You know what you could do, DICKHEAD! You could—*HEY, WATCH IT! WATCH WHAT YOU'RE DOING! HEY! HEY! DON'T PUT YOUR HANDS ON ME! DO NOT PUT YOUR HANDS ON ME! O.K! O.K! O.K! O.K! DO NOT PUT YOUR HANDS ON ME! YOU CRAZY!* ARE YOU CRAZY? I'll leave. Now I said I'll leave, and I'll leave. I'll leave. O.K! O.K! I'll leave! But don't do that! Don't you ever do that! Hear me! Don't you EVER put your hands on me! O.K! Put your hands on me again and I'll—Look! I'll leave! I'll leave!

YOU GOT ALL THE ROOM IN THE WORLD! Don't keep honking your horn! Just watch how you drive. Nobody is in your way. Just watch how you drive! Idiot! Bartender got smart at the mouth back there, didn't he! Screw the Yankees! Must be crazy! Reached for a baseball bat! He seemed ready to use it too! Oh, Yea! Well, still not so ready, I don't think—not at all, that I couldn't, that I couldn't if, I wanted to, go back there right now and turn his lights out for him! I don't give shit what he got tattooed on his arm! Yankees! Whoever! I don't give a shit! What syllables would escapes his lips, I'd like to know; how smart he would be still, I might wonder, if finding it difficult to breathe one night along a darkened way, he violently gasped and gasped again, quickly to savor, not the air he so desperately needed, but the stifling slime and froth of his own blood! So what if I didn't pay for one stinking drink—he knows who I am! He knows damn well who I am! All he had to do was put it on the tab! This is not the first time I've had a problem with this guy. He's always angry! Perhaps it was about more than just the drinks. Maybe there was something else. Maybe there was another incident. My memory's been playing tricks on me. Maybe I owe him from a previous. Maybe I forgot to pay. Maybe he doesn't think he should remind me. Maybe I don't owe him a Goddamn thing! How about that! How about that, eh! That still doesn't give him the right to put his hands on me! Nothing does! A knife to his throat, he'd squeal like a pig. Squeal like a Goddamn pig, he would! Piece of shit! He don't know who he's messing with! Believe me, he just doesn't know! Piece of shit!

Earlier on, I did something that might explain—that might be the key to all that transpired tonight. Over in the city, I drifted around aimlessly, until I ended-up in one of my old hangout-and-get-high neighborhoods. I should have known better! I bought—well, I was given some stuff sort of—thought zip-nothing of doing it, right there in the street, not a very smart move! There's a lot of funny shit going around, these days, a lot of funny stuff; amphetamines, speed—bad-speed, white-boy shit! I don't like speed. And I have a feeling that's what's inside me right now. I could feel it! Now that I'm out in the fresh

air, now that I'm in the street again, I could feel it taking over. I could feel myself being not quite in control.
In the bar I was talking loudly, more loudly than I realized—much more loudly than was necessary. Even among
the hard-core regulars, people were shying away, and giving me funny looks. No doubt about it, I was loud. Dope-
dealers do dumb shit sometimes, don't they! They sell you
whatever they feel like selling you. I should have known
better—I, of all people! God, I used to sell the shit myself, not so long ago! What time is it! Silvia's awake still.
She hates it when I'm messed-up like this! *(Stop using the
stuff! Why don't you just stop using the goddamn stuff!)* If
only it were that easy! Hold up! Wait a minute! Where am
I? Let's see! This is not good! God, sometimes I am unable
to tell whether I'm coming or going, to determine even
right from left! O.K! Let's pull ourselves together here!
Pull our selves together! Pigalle. Place Pigalle is back that
way. Gabby & Hayes. No, that's the other way. The Rue
Saint what-you-may-call-it runs parallel to this one, runs
parallel then—then a little further-on, a little further-on,
it cuts, it either cuts across—no: that's before it reaches,
before it reaches, I mean before it runs pass the sprawling
exterior of Peter's *Café du Mal.* I'm glad it isn't summer!
Paris is humid as hell in summer. It's got to be this way!
Gabby & Hayes. Yes, this way! The hotel's not far. . .not
far from . . . Wait a minute! WHAT am I thinking! Well
I'll be! I don't believe it! Here we go again! Off to the
races! What the hell's the matter with me! For a minute
back there I thought I actually was in Paris. I don't believe
it! I must have been dreaming on my feet—walking and
dreaming and thinking still, as sometimes happens! Paris
of all places! I starved in Paris! Am I losing my mind! *(Of
course, you're losing your mind! What else is new!)* What
else? Nothing. Nothing apparently, except that. . .except
that now (oh, that's nice) some sick bastard, some freaking
son of a creep, could for whatever his reasoning, find no

better use of his time (apparently) than to be following me. He'd better not be following me, the mood I'm in right now! He'd better not be! He's not—yes he is! No, he isn't! Look at that! He's pretending to be having trouble with his front-door key. Now he's ringing somebody's bell. Who's he trying to kid! He doesn't live in that building! He's trying the key again. He doesn't—oh shit, he does, he does live in the building! Maybe he wasn't following me after-all! I'm losing it! I'm losing it, man! The bartender was up to something, though—I mean starting an argument over the drinks! Bob—no, pardon me, *Baab! Baab* ordered this drink! *Baab* ordered that drink! *Baab! Baab! Baab!* Who the hell is *Baab!* I don't know no goddamn *Baab!* I don't think he even gave me my correct change. Baab, my ass! I should have more money in my pocket. Then there was that fella at the corner of the bar, I didn't like the looks of. He kept turning his back. He kept watching me sideways. I had the feeling he was trying to listen to what I was saying. He might have been taking notes. Now all of a sudden—all of a sudden for no reason I could think of, I'm (nauseous?)

The last drink tasted funny. It might be the drinks. It could be the culmination of several things: shit from earlier on in the day, not mixing well with other stuff floating around in my system, I don't know. Check this, though! A face you've never seen before is out on the block. His shit is *D-zope* (or, so says someone, someone who heard it from someone, who got it from someone else). We all know how that story go—sometimes it's reliable, sometimes it isn't! Anyway, he wouldn't even talk to anyone he doesn't know. He's adamant about not taking a short. He singles you out—never seen you before, but singles you out, lets you have a bag for next to nothing; doesn't count the money (and it was short), just shoves it in his shirt! What was that all about? That right there should have raised a flag. That by itself should have told you something! You're taking a chance with your life when you put substance you obtain from a total stranger, be it pills, powder, liquid, into your system; even when legally-prescribed, you're still not sure. You're playing Russian roulette. Most of the time, you're playing Russian roulette, and don't even know it. I remember reading about an experiment, in which some type of opiate was given to a dozen or so 'volunteers' at a 'safe house' or 'undisclosed' location here in the city somewhere. Dr. Zimmerman looked nervous as hell when he saw the manila folder in my hands. (The loose-leaf file was among others atop one of the file-cabinets in the shelter. How was I to know that it was off-limits.) The 'safe house' and 'undisclosed' location might be, the subjects who 'volunteered', may well have been, who knows, close enough to home, that it made him uncomfortable! Naturally, I didn't get far before he had someone remove the folder from my hands! But the little I read left me thinking, still. The subjects had a variety of reactions, but were mainly 'delusional' and 'disoriented'; some thought shadows were people, that with spirits conjoined, they were themselves not one, but multiple individuals, and roamed the streets—imagined they were roaming the streets—in the company of like-others, who remained non-visible to all but themselves, asleep and awake and dreaming at the same time, in a never-ending half-night. Others at first were furious and threatening, before becoming melancholy and uncommunicative. One or two believed themselves guilty of crimes they could not—not by any stretch of the imagination—have committed (torture-murders inside World War II German prison camps, drowning of women at locations they were unable to pinpoint beyond phrases such as, 'over there' and that, 'it was in the dark', and the like). I don't trust Zimmernan! What's literature like that doing in a shelter for homeless persons! All the same, roaming the streets, in my present state of mind, is not good. I don't trust myself! I need some kind of counseling. I need to calm down. A good cognac would do it. That piece-of-shit fool of a bartender—all I needed was one drink! *Piece of shit!* One of those twenty milligrams joints (the tablets that what's-his-name sells) might be better. What's his name? I could never think of his name! Anyway, right now his name is of no consequence. His shit works, and that's all that matters. But even if I had the ten dollars, I still would have to find him. He's at the Mickey D's up from the shelter during the day, but this time of night, I don't know. These days, people are not letting-go of their medically-prescribed medication the way they used to. They might want fifteen, they might want twenty dollars. Twenty dollars! Where would I get twenty dollars at this time of night!

I say! I say! 'Scuse me! 'Scuse me, sa! Don't mean ta-be ah buddah! Don't mean ta-be ah buddah! But you. . .you wouldn't 'appen ta 'av a si-gah-rrret, would you! Ah si-gah-rrret! Would you please, sa! Aaaaaah! 'Ow d'ya like that! 'Ow d'ya like that! 'Taar!

Counseling I don't need, any more than I need worthless medication, any more than I need to be buying stuff in the street, or anywhere else for that matter. *(I hate the taste of menthol! How can anyone smoke these things! They taste like shit!)* Anyway, the idea that a user of substance, even a casual one, could diagnose—let alone medicate—himself, is a dangerous one. Still, I know my body better than anyone else. The bag I got earlier-on was pure (or contained at least a percentage of) speed! Nobody could tell me different. Now I need something that would calm me down. Speed does the opposite. Apart from leaving me with a hammer in my head (which could last from one day going into the next), speed scrambles my thoughts. My mind is racing. I need a cigarette. I must have a cigarette! Normally I don't smoke. Normally I won't go near a cigarette. *Speed!* As a rule, I'm more partial to, more comfortable with, how should I put it, 'a mellower type' high. The warming weightlessness, and near-airborne glide immediately following the downing of a stiff cognac — now that's for me! Speed is different; it expands my perception, yes. It sharpens my focus that sometimes, oblivious of all else, I'm locked in debate with myself, reviewing issues I would otherwise hardly ever pay attention to; yet it does so in such a frenzied and disarrayed manner, that by episode's end, which could be hours (sometimes even days) later, the few bright passages, the seemingly non-stop revelations are no longer as lucid (and, of course, makes hardly as much sense) as when they were emblazoned across the monitor of my mind, at the intense higher-points of the drug's influence. That's not good. It's not good to find yourself on trails hopelessly locked, without an understanding as to where your tracks would lead, or as to what got you started in a certain direction in the first place; to be by random thoughts propelled every which way, along lanes of confusion and uncertainty, is not good. At times I am disoriented. Occasionally I blank-out. There are gaps — permanent gaps — in my memory. I sometimes lose my sense of direction. I am convinced sometimes, that I am a soldier — an invisible soldier — behind enemy lines, on an expanse of desolate terrain (the surface perhaps of another planet), in pursuit of a legion of diminutive near-humans in futuristic space-gear, a voice in my head-set (my commanding-officer's, I guess) imploring: *Attack! Kill! Destroy!* Sometimes I need to be reacquainted with things others take for granted, things I myself long ago took for granted, some of the very things the radio-host, and his callers-in were getting excited about during this morning, or was it now yesterday's — or perhaps another morning's transmission, I'm not sure. Perhaps this happens every day, every day at the same time of day. Perhaps I can't tell one day from the next. I'm already having trouble linking groups of people to tracts of land, distin-

guishing state from country, country from nation, nation
from people, that sort of thing. And of course I have no
idea which war (perhaps I should say whose war) our radio-host is referring to. Though, 'We'd be done', he
seemed to be saying, 'with those bastards in no time!'
Anyway, the difference between a state-of-war and a state
of woe eludes me. At one time, there used to be, I seem to
recall, a Department of War, or War Office or something
like that (in which, a Minister or Lord of war—or however you'd want to describe him—resided and ruled). If it
were those days still, I could have gone there and made
inquiries, and would have been able, later-on, to call-in
and relayed the answers (along with my own modifica-
tions or embellishments) to the radio station, just like any
normal citizen might have. Anyway, that's been long-gone
(the Department-of-War, I mean); war itself is still around,
of course. The transition from War Department to whatever it's called now was smooth. No contestant on no television quiz-show, ever recalled (not that one was ever
asked) on which night at midnight the change came into
effect, let alone the precise hour at which they tore down
the sign. No sir, that one, like an odorless fart in a noise-
filled room, its leave obsequious took, with nary an uneasy
moment for anyone within range. Still you would think
that the softening-up even of the phrase describing an office which managed so terrible an aspect of human enter-
prise as the business of war, would be (if only for the history books) a celebratory affair, a red-letter day; you'd
think there would be crowds in the street watching a bon-
fire of uniforms, the toppling of a monument here and
there, the (symbolic at least) destruction of some military
paraphernalia, a discarding one or two of medals, a general atop a bridge urinating into a river, things of that nature, something, some of the things we do when we are
triumphant and proud. Then, again maybe just as well.
The new Department (whatever it is called) does, I imag-

ine, a far more efficient job, than its predecessor might have, even if the revision had never occurred! This is futile! I don't know, maybe the act of war itself is futile! I mean what's with the camouflaging! What's with the naming and renaming! By any other name, armed-conflict (be it stones used as clubs, beer-bottles as missiles, a bolo to the enemy's brain, a clash of sabers, chemical poisoning, drones in the sky, laser-guided what-have-you, wide-scale government-sponsored epidemics), would only result in whatever extent and nature of blood-spill, injury, death, and hardship, the combatant parties are capable of inflicting upon each other (and themselves) at that particular point in time, wouldn't it! I'm normally not concerned, I don't get worked-up about much—certainly not about things upon which I'm in no position to affect a change. I must be speeding—speeding or losing my mind, or both! Madness in its myriad forms is grounded, they say, always in speed—in incoherence of thought, anyway. Hey, look! I ingest, I excrete, I'm sufficiently comfortable, not tied to a nine-to-five. I'm not on anybody's kill-list. Nothing throws me off. An act of sexual gratification here and there, be it most of the time, none more than the starring role in a brief one-man show—I'm good. A pain free end, dismembered and unremembered, non-eulogized, an unattended non-ceremony, lost-at sea, rot in peace, burn in hell; me ashes stored in a piss-pot or marble urn: No problem! But as to war, I still don't understand why, I don't understand why not, I mean—or even why everyone doesn't think about it all the time. I mean war is as inseparable a part of being a modern human as that area within our brains which drives us to procreate, or propels us, it seems, towards drugs and alcohol usage! It is the one first badge we should carry with us when we begin establishing colonies in space: that we are *makers of war!* But then again, perhaps it's the one badge, we shouldn't—and, of course do, in fact, possess the good sense, that we don't, and wouldn't! We are intelligent creatures, are we not? Just imagine if the pre-Colombians had known what was coming, had been forewarned, and (of consequence, worse still), strategically fore-armed! Boy, what a *Nuevo Mundo* that would have been! War is as much part of ourselves, as the air we breathe and the substance we excrete! Separated for more than a brief period from either of them we can never be. But the word, I don't know—I think with *war,* it is the word itself that troubles us. Even I could see that! Peculiar things, words! Once learned they forever deep within us reside, to chronicle sometimes our grievances; with matters of heart, an angry sea to churn of uncontrollable impulses. Apart from evoking disturbing images: a red-man's feathered-dress, barbaric hordes, Genghis Khan galloping across the steppes of Asia; assaults on the fields of opium; Tokyo Joe in the cockpit of a propeller plane, Tokyo Rose poisoning the airwaves; Halls of Montezuma/ Shores of Tripoli, Shaka Zulu, the Saracens, Capone and his mob, teenage gang-members wearing pompadours and carrying shivs—the word *war* brings to mind all kinds of unpleasant things: thoughts of infanticide and rape (inevitable, let's face it, during periods of military occupancy); looting, plundering, priceless cultural artifacts being stolen or destroyed; sickos of the species, madmen given free reign, desaparecidos, necrophiliacs, corpses desecrated, Nazis in Europe, brains gone wrong; Rum and Coca-cola mother/daughter prostitutes! Wow, we should be careful with words. They are not that easy to regulate. Maybe (bearing in mind that they are accessible to all), we should regard them the same way we regard explosives and fire: essential, but capable of causing terrible things to happen.

III

O heinous crimes! Vile words! Foul murder! Mischief! May-
hem! Within whose hearts you reside! Before a head-count
is taken, before even a pulse is checked to determine wheth-
er someone actually died; even without a body of evidence,
you are of vengeful cries. After the completion of a gallows
the furor seldom subsides. Indeed that's when things are at
their hysterical worst (or best, whichever way you want to
look at it). People are trampled to death in the crowds that
mill at the thought of executions, floggings, and the like.
Near these sights, there is always, confusion, a confluence,
a torrent, words . . .

It was handy, it was neat, and serving the wearer well,
concealed his identity, the bandanna across the bridge of
his nose; though it alerted us (admittedly usually too late),
that he at least existed. We saw the weapon he carried, and
imagined the ramparts we would build. Life was simpler
then. Squares of fabric into triangles folded, as face-masks
these days obscure but items in flea-markets and amuse-
ment parks and carnivals; there-placed often-times by
hands idle and frivolous. In the making of movies, costu-
miers and scenarists have little use for them. Gone by way
of the cap-pistol, a device unheard of it remains today,
even among young kids at play. Discomforting no more
than the wooden red-skins of old-fashioned drugstores,
our space-age waylayers, having under-gone a lifting of

face and change of name, are (along with the purveyors of deception and murder) regarded less-hysterically intolerably than were their earlier counterparts. Sophisticated now more, no longer 'common' thieves, they inoculate their victims with amesmering imagery from within clever trance-inducing PR campaigns; helped occasional by a prod (the threat at least of such) from the stick of the State (with whom, not many of us realize, they arc but not-so-distant, sometimes feuding cousins sort-of); their apparel of villainy discarded, they lament, they might as well lament, that they are simply maintaining their life-styles (which, of course, they are!) We see them on television. They are of disaster relief. They smile on camera. They help win elections. They sit comfortably in high office. But that's as far as we get. Hey, the days when people met face to face, shook hands, were introduced, and thereafter 'knew' each other; when a head-of-state and his spouse, would smile at well-wishers while waiting in line (even in the dead of winter) for seats at the local cinema, are long gone. Close to a century after Lincoln's unguarded walk to the theater, the new-usurpers fearing that the true depths of their subterfuge might be gauged, remained cautious still of taking full advantage of the leverage they secretly possessed. They've shifted gears! Starting with a slaying in Sweden, they more comfortably began ridding themselves of the remaining vestiges of that earlier shyness! Olof Palme! Ah yes, Palme! How tidy an act that was! Not even a feasible motive! Aren't they the best ones though, the murders without motives, that remain unsolved and forgotten, while the bastards who had them committed get elected to high office, given immunity from prosecution at worse! But let's not fuss! Let's not get exited! Murder is murder—we all know that! Alright! Murder is as murder murders. Olof's was sweet. It was sweet and it was foul. It was as sweet as it was foul! Let's leave it alone! Dark hearts that planned it well, rejoice! You've won that one! 'Now they are as frightened as we've all along *pretended to be,*' you can in secret say! Hey! To whoever orchestrates these slayings, an award! Whatever you choose to call it, hand it to him, (not on television, of course) but hand it to him, please! Whether you abhor murder or not, admit it, the slaying in Sweden of Olof Palme was a beaut, wasn't it! Booth may have had to run like a dog in the night, sullying the name even of the physician who attended him, but the big hand when it stamped that one in Stockholm: NOT TO BE SOLVED, embossed it good and well for all of time! Nowadays not even a hot-shot television-newscaster, or Johnny-come-greatly talk-show host, not even while consensus man-dates, (and in the third person referring to himself, he repeatedly insists) that you with familiarity address him, would even contemplate walking the street without be-ing protected by some form of camouflaging, or identi-ty-obscuring device, be it a purposefully badly-tailored suit, a pair of dark-glasses the size of saucers, a Bozo-the-clown's outfit (on his way to a 'charity-for-kids' event), a now-you-see-me/now-you-don't lighthearted staged af-fair (from which, with heavy security, he'll be whisked in and out); a giant blown-up photograph, a larger than life-sized effigy of himself, a huge logo of the television channel corporation home-base out of which he address-es his following of fans, God knows what else. Beyond his entourage, the electronic moat of his 'comfort zone', his pricey up-scaled residence, let us not even set eyes! Forget about his legions of hysterical fans and courtiers and bodyguards! Now this is perplexing! It really is! You would think that the fact that so widespread and numerous a conglomeration of clans—their well-wishers, clamor-ing alignavecs, servants and spies—could, at this point in time, so successfully technically blatantly 'shield' them-selves; that their getting away with it for so long, might cause an uproar! What with the veil, even the headscarf (don't even mention the burka or hoodie) regarded of late as being so passionately offensive (more egregious, mind you, with each passing day), you would think there would at least be a public outcry—riots, demonstrations, editorials in prestigious magazines and newspapers, and so on! Wrong. Wrong. Wrong. Wrong. Wrong. No one bats an eye! Don't you know that people nowadays look forward to—enjoy, actually enjoy, and would decry others who didn't appreciate—being shoved violently out of the way to make room for their betters! Hoping for a glimpse of their favorite newscaster, the faithful in front of television studios, dutifully daily already stand hours long behind the barricades! Ever wondered why the plight of certain individuals, some you might even know and love (befallen of criminal bloodshed, lost-of-limb, a family member murdered, or some equally tragic misfortune) isn't making the news you're watching, and remains unnoticed even by its presenters, while some genital in a suit and tie waxes *ad absurdum* about the starlet beside him; with, off-camera at the controls, the blokes who decide these matters, weighing frantic of her patterned-toenails, the close-up more suitable for the millions awaiting this type data, they should transmit! Ever wondered—ever wondered why no-one cares! This is a joke! This is all a joke, you're thinking, some sort of distortion of facts! Let's try an experiment! Stand completely motionless, look intently silently long at someone out of, say, law-enforcement (bearing in mind that they are not that high up on the totem-pole), the next time you're out in the streets. At the same time hold in your mouth a few small objects, buttons or shelled-walnuts, something like that—so that when you are confronted, your speech would be (well, somewhat declamatory and garbled—foreign better still, not from around here-ish). See what happens! Try this experiment, and when you've finished, without revealing the outcome, just for the hell of it, suggest to someone else that he does the same—No! No, please don't! That wouldn't be cool. Reckless we must never become! Like any other well-trained breed of canine, the *doggas* instinctively know whose hands to lick, around whose feet to whine and yelp, which throat to 'collar', or sink their teeth into, whose lights they could with impunity blatantly put out.

Of course upper echelon tribes (their militarists, apologists, media priests, high-priestesses, and concubines) are seldom taken to task! As to how much skin, genitalia, he or she (their spouses, their offspring) choose; where and when, on camera or off, to expose or cover, celebrities are never questioned! Theirs is contract, a not surprising symbiosis, super-celeb with super-state, one validating the other; one consecrating the other! Close together they always will stand. Look! Let's say even that, continuously painful evidence of their transgressions had reached the tip of our nostrils, was staring down our throats; copteron urinated on our dead, dumped their toxic waste into the with-excrement-already-crested river, on which we for subsistence still depend; their drones indiscriminately nightly turned breathing living beings into waste—with our backs against the wall, and their sabers permanently at our throats, what would a sensible maneuver be? Please don't mention, *rights!* Isn't it futile even to debate the question of (and we're back to words here again) rights, with those who from jump take the position (and have the wherewithal, remember, the brute-force if need be, to defend it), that *their* rights are non-disputable, believing their fortresses (at the same time) unassailable, and that the patches of ground within them, sacred forever will remain! (How well Andrew Jackson understood this! It is not for nothing that they called him *the Devil,* you know!) Think of the packs of well-trained hounds, let alone those running wild, silent and wild! Consider the legions of undercover horn-blowers! Enlistees from any one of a number of secret militias (whose current collective murders must number already, God alone knows, how many tens of thousands) could be sitting next to you right now in a bar or restaurant. They listen to your conversation. They could, while your back is turned, be emptying the contents of a capsule into your drink; you'd never notice. Discomforting prospects, even under the best of circumstance, the conjoined-spirits of non-visibility and anonymity, embodied in a single individual, or group of individuals, portend of a near-divine omniscience, do they not! Who's minding the store while your back is turned! As you speak these days, who's holding the telephone! Imagine individuals far away determining that you are to be zapped from the sky; and that, in the future, they would most likely do so, leaving no more evidence than the traces of a heart-attack (assuming, that is, that by then there would be need still that they cover their tracks!) Think about it! Could it be they are scaled-down, secretly-imagined, halfway-towards becoming; about any moment now to exit the closets, declaring themselves (or, as is more excitingly fashionable these days), getting themselves elected, Gods! Yea, Gods! Alright then, Gods of a sort—not quite Ja but Jaduka; Rawan more than Ram; Ramses not Ra; less Julius Caesar than Prete Gianni; more Santa Babara than Shango—you get my drift! *The Truncheons* and the *Scalpel-balms* hold us at bay: armed one with a reservoir of brute-force; the other, with the threatened withholding of its life-sustaining special skills. (Of these henchman gangs, before letting-go of Algeria, the French make excellent use, didn't they!) To the bloodying, black-hooding, and torturing of our fellow-creatures, we are not averse, they'll say. Electric drills are at the ready for the knee-caps of those who would be defiant. The choice is yours, they'll say. Conform or be Coerced, the banners will read! Comply or be vilified! Even if they were in a media-wide scandalous way exposed (and this, unlikely), the majority of world authorities and legal scholars, determined their behavior to be outrageous, egregious, and criminal (this unlikely too), not much will come of it; things would remain 'non-reviewable' still, 'taken care of'; treated as if they never happened, a marriage by Pope-and-Church-annulled, a presidential-pardon sort-of-thing. Blame would be elsewhere relegated. Ours would suddenly be a heavier load to tote. *So yuz got a big mouth, they'd say! Yuz got a big mouth, have yuz! Had yuz bowed your heads, as was respectful to do, they'd say, yuz would not have seen what yuz thought was your father's ghost at midnight! Yuz would not have been able to draw attention to his demise! Yuz would have noticed not even the dew on the leaves in the moonlight! Hey, we know, we've long known how to deal with your kind, they'd say; we've always known! We've always known!*

As to whose hands you shake, take care! Genetically-engineered near-humans, excreting miniscule lethal doses of venom by way of their finger-tips, among us daily mingle! Watch for the poison they spit! Once the image of you dead, or for whatever reason, in solitary till dead confined, appears on the in-brain monitors within the secret rooms of certain groups of 'powerful' individuals, you're never mind the bollocks more times than not, as good as deceased; descended into the depths already even of hell. Another story, a different kettle of fish, our concern as to our own well-being, our complaints that we're being railroaded, getting not a fair shake; our dropping like flies, even though occurring for centuries, is but an illusion (one supported by statistics and logic) we are told. The ethnic groups that numbered millions and vanished, the unearthed graves, piled corpses, mangled limbs, eyes melted in their sockets, are our 'own doing' at worse; we are paranoids, ill-informed, delusional, uneducated, superstitious; conceived most of the time out of wedlock, we sprout off-the-wall religions, pray to the wrong gods;

even before we spew from the womb, we are illegal, we enter life's fray with a record. We become career-criminals, prone to illicit drug-use. We are mired in a black past, prejudiced—racist even (that is, if the term carries any real meaning still). One night, in the shelter, I was out of sorts, all nerves; I politely asked if someone would look through the venetian blinds to see if a young man was standing in the shadows across the street. (He had been following me.) How Dr. Zimmerman learned of my request, I have no idea. But he immediately became enraged. He would have none of it! He all but sprang from his chair, removed his glasses, and with his eyes alone, forbade that anyone should assist me. When he reached for his blood/alcohol-level testing-kit, everyone in the shelter seemed to know that I would be first in line. From that night on, I kept (I tried to keep) personal ideas to myself. I really tried. Yet mine for some reason continued—continues, I don't know why, to this day still—to be a host of troubling habits: standing up for the under-dog, speaking my mind, continuing to raise my voice, even when told repeatedly to be silent; refusing to placate the law-abides (when I full well know that they'll have the doggas on me at the drop of a hat). O.K! So it's a *mondo cane,* so it's every man for himself, things off-kilter, a planet hurtling dangerously rapidly out of control; a savage world (of which I can't say that I and others like myself did not in its creating partake); that I alone my share of dirt and more contributed, I don't deny. But even so, whose blood I shed that they would hold me enemy this day still! What reason could there be for my being targeted! My current crimes are so few, so petty in nature, they would hardly a blip cause to appear on a single monitor in the Bureau of Criminal Offenses, on the screens in any of the watchdog agencies (of which nowadays there are, God alone knows, how many) maintaining a round-the-clock vigil, even of every square millimeter of the planet's surface. My motto is—has always been: *Chu unu! Chu every las wan ah unu!* I'm no threat. No-one could ever accuse me of taking sides. Who could I betray, except myself (and haven't I well over a thousand times already done so!) I know no sovereignty, honor no home, nor fatherland. I recognize no Anthem. I don't own a passport, or carry identification of any kind; I tell people I was born on the island of Tristan *Da Cuna* (which sank, I believe, to the ocean floor well over a half-century ago); I salute no flag—bear allegiance to none! I constantly diligently reexamine my feelings to make sure that I maintain with the same intensity, the level of abhorrence I've always carried for everyone of the world's high flying bastards; that I'm not prejudice, that I regard none in disfavor than the others less, I'm always on guard. In wartime (which, is all the time, in case you didn't know), I detest opposing generals (and Heads of States) equally. I've never voted. Shouldn't these attributes entitle me to something—me name on a scrap of tissue I could paste, if even only with the turd of me award, on a wall somewhere; immunity from prosecution (well, for minor offenses), exemption from deportation (or me name positioned at least way down on the bottom half of the list); a jumping of the turnstiles, a ride around the city every now and then, the Department of Public Transport picking-up the tab, things of that nature—how about it! Come on! How about it! What loss suffered if some of these conditions—even if all of these conditions—are agreed upon! What loss! How much more hardship would the world endure if, in addition to all its ails, I dreamed now often of Sodom (or worse), while thinking at the same time of some upper-crust industrialist, politician, or financier's tender young daughter, whose photographs regularly provocatively appeared in magazines and on television; and, let's say—miraculously, charitably—she entertained me, Ah, yes, let's say that she did, catered to my every whim, allowed me my excesses! How damaging the hurt! Wherefore the tragedy! What have I done lately that anyone other than those with whom I come in daily contact (at best, a sorry bunch, if you asked me) let alone the creatures who walk around with the scowled faces of authority, and the mark of death at the end of their felt pens), would even know I existed. Let's get serious! When you think about it—when you really think about it, this is what it amounts to: Anyone who holds ideas that run contrary to the beliefs of those currently in control, and dares to speak on them, does so at his own peril. If he expresses himself loudly enough, adeptly enough, amplify his feelings by the way of a not-yet-roped-in news agency, sing them atop a minaret (made use even of a common bullhorn), so that others would take notice; if he caused any kind of stir, he could find himself no matter who he is, Mwna Mutapa, King Ja Ja, the Za-ana-Yamani; local or foreign, illustrious or chorten; Panjab, Wahab, riddle-raddle Deutch, Aborigine; dressed in a kapara, wearing a suit and tie or toga, nothing but a stringed half-a-coconut shell that cupped his genitals; his mother, Maliket Saba— it matters not who, what language he speaks, what he looks like or where he came from, he could find himself (don't even mention being dark skinned and non-christian) in the cross-hairs of a posse immune from prosecution, the eighty percent, (we're guessing here) white; your prosthetic arms and legs bet, no shortage of happy-to-serve black mikky-fikkys among the remaining twenty per cent (or in line, waiting at least, to join), best-in-the-world—they're not shy, they'll tell you themselves— official kill-squad murderers (KSWADM?) of the day. This much I'm sure everyone knows. Still what role besides that of an out-of-focus anonymous *restavec* among an insignificant random tribe of new-age drug-abusing roma nomads, could mine be! Perhaps I really have nothing to fear, nothing to worry about, except my brain which refuses to be still (and that much I've always been aware of). Perhaps no one is targeting me. I might be wrong. I might be wrong about everything (it won't be the first time!) Maybe I'm up to my old tricks again, off to the races, scaring myself, scaring others, foaming at the mouth, high on speed, high on coke; attempting to unravel a mystery, to solve a puzzle, without determining whether or not a puzzle existed, or that a mystery should unravel, in the first place (or whether I would, one way or the other, benefit from any one of these endeavors); not minding my own business, looking at life (as I do often) ass-backwards, so to speak; ruffling feathers; hearing voices; seeing things, hearing things, speaking in tongues, speaking in 'unknown' tongues, claiming to hold 'secrets', claiming to know the secret of, A *ban and a skun and a skun and a dan! SKUNANADAN! SKUNANADAN! SKUNANADAN!* I'm bugging! Yes, I'm *bugging!* I'm not! Really, I'm *not!* O.K! O.K! *Splatam! Splatam Splut! Atuluma! Atuluma Huluma! BUNGA! BUNGA! BUNGA!* Sorry! Yes! No. Yes. I'm not bugging, I tell you, I'm not! I'm not! O.K! O.K! O.K! Beside the point! Look! Cha! DAMN IT, MAN! Never mind me! Draw your own line! Draw your own line in the sand! See what those bastards on the other side are up to! God, they've already almost all the way succeeded! This is what transpired: They simply (like pinning a ribbon, like pinning the same color ribbon on every tree in the forest, on every tree in every forest), over the years made sure that every home everywhere had been converted into a Dr. Pavlov's laboratory. They fitted them all with mirrors, mirrors and bells, light and sound, the crackle never far, of gunfire!) What do you think the screen on your television set is! Even in the most impoverished of neighborhoods in the most rundown ghetto on the planet, you're sure to find them in great numbers! Why do you think they are so readily in excellent working condition discarded! Walk the streets long enough in any of the major cities in the more affluent countries, you'll find one! This is an accident, you think? O.K! So they inundated the world with television-sets, then filled them with continuous provocative images, with repetitive, rhythm-based music, with jovial hosts, clean-shaved suit-and-tied newscasters making silly jokes, insipid women, staccato gunfire, sirens and screams; top-of-the-charts babble (jihadists, cross-of-Jesus onward-Christian-soldiers marching 'as to' war); big-money giveaways, rags-to-riches idiocy, made-up-to-the-gills hysterical female judges presiding over cock-a-mammy court-room dramas; damsels in distress, their genital areas shrinking of pubic hairs; the blood-gush and *kersplatt* of kill-moments, the screech of tires, canned anonymous laughter; at regular almost predictable intervals, a dehumanized enemy (an every-so-often view of humans made tiny like insects by way of copter-cams in the sky); dark-haired Fu Manchu Ali Baba Eastern European mustachioed types, autopsies, de-empathizing kill-games, body-bags, corpses, sirens and screams, God knows whatever; each with its particular slot, designed and structured to appear at the same time of day, everyday, everyday, everyday, everywhere! More seriously. More seriously now, let's get a little more serious now: sandwiched between all this, *De News! Wow. Mani! Mani! Get ya daily dose now! Wa y'a say? Mani, me nar a say a Gaddamn ting! Get ya own bludklat news!* You are worried that the person next to you could be 'miked', you are being monitored, your home might be bugged! Don't be silly! Why would they waste their time doing something like that! Why would that even be necessary? You regularly watch your favorite television shows, don't you? You've already been cut-off at the pass! All they need do now is extrapolate. They know how you think. You go to the library or bookstore, don't you! What are you reading! You own an electronic-device? Everyone does nowadays!

Simple as pie! In the line of this type fire, blitz in this manner, it's not easy for you to regard yourself and those around you with reasonable scrutiny; to in any systemic way, ascertain who you are, who you really are; whether you are human, or a cleverly assembled *syntheticon* walking around thinking that you are; that you're as normal as everybody-else is not so easily determined! Of course, you're never sure, you'll never be sure of anything! The stranger avoiding your gaze in the pale dawn light might *kani-gianni* only be, the happenstance-earlier privileged *mbakara* of an innocent (and by others, noticed hardly) encounter, of the local *kswadm* unlikely; but Jizzo, izzor dizzor diznary Jizzo Blizzo; with, ya'd never know, the casualness and flavor of a walk-dog morning, drenched and disguised; a morning timorously tortuously trying to free itself from its own spew, of which now you are constituent! What was the fellow's purpose? What in the first place was the cause of his (and your own) discomfort, and discontent? Was it simply a discrepancy to do with the purchase of a pill, or tiny envelope containing a powdered substance that cost ten dollars and failed to do, that always fails to do, exactly as it's supposed to do; a drug transaction gone wrong, the delayed adverse effects of shit in your system, the faulty forceps with which you were extracted from the womb, the planet, moon, and stars at the precise moment of your birth, fatally aligned; or of a thousands things, of which by itself any single one, could have been responsible for your being 'mentally challenged', not up to speed; not being able to make sense of your surroundings, unable to determine, even if it meant saving your life, whether the liquid damp that cloaks you now is the Seine in Paris, the Hudson skirting a New Jersey town, or the Tyrrhenian near Corsica. It's not easy, not with all the whacked-up speed and whatever else untested experimental substances, (over-the-counter or bootlegged; illicit or complicit, home-grown or foreign) fermenting within your system, entering your bloodstream, day after day after day, racing through the conduit of your veins and arteries; dissolving, coagulating, dissolving again, a becoming-stronger-as-they-barrel company of poisonous units, heading in the direction of, soon to link-up with, the legions of encamped venom, in a well-on-the-way campaign, an advance-guard devastating even further, the already deteriorating circuitry of your ill-functioning, near-exhausted, dead-soon brain . . .

IV

Entry: Stand up! Stand up! What garbage! Is this unfath-
omable inhospitable place still Rome! Stand up! What un-
bearable stench! Am I too now haphazard flesh and blood
upon these stones, amid this squalor, helpless of these
rebellious thoughts that, jostling with others seditious
and pale, dance a J'overt morning's abandon within the
caverns of my mind; an out-of-carnival's dress-rehearsal
forlorn frightful figure that dozed through it all unaware;
unaware somehow that he'd not only with his presence,
darkened the corner at which he stood, but that of the dark
itself, monarch too suddenly he had become! Rome had
fallen, the parade ended, the reveling crowds come and
gone; ash-Wednesday was wide-awake, the festival's de-
mons, purposefully-lagged, angrily tormented him: Pay de
Devil! Pay de Devil! Pay de Devil!

Waaat! Waaat! O. Kay! O.K. I'm awake. I am asleep.
I am not asleep. I am half-asleep. I wasn't asleep.
Look! Even if I was, even if I was asleep—anyway, I'm
not asleep. I'm not asleep now, am I! Am I? Very well,
then. Give us a break, then! Give us a break! *(Lazarus
will rise!)* Yes. Yes. Yes. Cognac! Cognac it was! Yes. Yes.
Yes. In the course of the last several hours, I'll say. Yes,
I'll say I knocked back a few! Sure did! *Yes! Yes! Yes!*
Memory serving me correctly, good cognac it was too. I
didn't break any laws in so doing, did I? Of a disturbance

am I aware, you say? That took place earlier on, you say? Not that I recall—I don't think so! No! *(I guess Lazarus is more than risen now!)* Hey, I'm not a deputy. I'm not in any way to the maintenance of order-and-law affiliated. Mine isn't the responsibility to determine whether the person (or persons) standing next to me is in violation or not! That responsibility is yours, I dare say, since you're the accepted custodian for the cylinders of lead that are standard in the righting of wrongs around here. And, yes—yes, I know what these damp patches near the crotch on the front of my trousers look like. Thank you for reminding me! Believe what you will, they are the result of a mishap which occurred a short while ago on this very street; on this very street, yes. Some idiot drove his SUV into a pool of water, and in so doing, caused a group of at-the-intersection pedestrians (me among them) to be drenched, an elderly couple receiving the brunt of the assault, the old-boy going almost into convulsions as he shook his fists and swore at the figure behind the wheel. Quite a scene, it was! An irate youngster wanted with his skateboard to make a dent on the passenger-side door, but the lights had changed, with the vehicle already speeding away, before he could affect any kind of damage. That's it, as far as I remember. I can't think of anything else.

Wait! Wait a minute! Something did happen. Yes! Something happened earlier-on at one of the bars! Yes, there was an altercation—no: I take that back! Scratch that last statement! I don't want to be inaccurate or misleading. Let's just say that for a ten minute (maybe a fifteen minute or so) period, things became untidy. Yes. Yes, I'm more comfortable describing it in such terms! Let me see! Let me see, now! What happened! A group of young people, absorbed in what at first seemed an academic or political debate, suddenly found themselves in a heated tug-o-war of words, which escalated into a trading of insults and jeers, interspersed with the occasional loud threat of violence, accompanied by derisive laughter and cat-calls and cries. This continued unabated for a while, getting louder and louder, until the sound of breaking glass became signal-apparent for one of the bartender/bouncers that he should intervene; a stout fellow, Bob — Bob Bagwell, I think his name was. They call him 'Babbet', or something like that, for short. I kind of know him personally. Anyway, he quickly appeared, singling-out and requesting of several individuals that they vacate the premises — which they did (he stood like a mastiff among them) without the protestations as would normally erupt in cases such as these. Before the shit quieted, I remember now, some old bag of a lesbian had the nerve to accuse me (Imagine!) of 'coming on' to her girlfriend. Give me a break! Give me a — wait, no! I tell a lie! I tell a lie! That was at another bar and, I think, another night. I'm getting a little off-track here. I'm sorry! Anyway as to the subject at hand, I still wouldn't use the word *disturbance* (certainly not in the legal sense) to describe anything that happened during that brief period, typical Saturday night stuff that was, no more. I'd almost forgotten until now, even that anything had taken place. And, you know, looking back, I certainly don't see that it merits any kind of official inquiry or review. I — Whoa! Hey! Hey, I'm sorry! O.K! O.K. I'm sorry! You're right! You're quite right! I should be more concerned, you're quite right, with explaining my own irrational behavior — my own alleged irrational behavior, I might add — with justifying perhaps even my presence on this particular street, in this particular part of town, at this time of night, I know, I know — rather than trying to tell you how to do your job. You're quite right! Once again, you're right! Forgive me! I was trying to say that . . . I . . . live . . . in the shelter. Anyway, the problem, my problem is: unable most of the time to with confidence rely on memory, I am, as a result, usually at a loss defending myself against accusations random and spurious, even as the ones I suspect I'm

about to be hit with any minute now. Still, it's not so much
that I fail to remember events, as much as being unable
sometimes to accurately determine the sequence in which
they occurred. Things that happen not yet even a half an
hour past, are from my memory (sometimes permanently,
it would seem) erased, or become juxtaposed with imaginary others, or those even which may have occurred on
different occasions (years apart sometimes) and at different places. But by the same token, let me point-out, that in
other aspects, my ability to recall is excellent—excellent
well, I say! Last year! Last year's warm weather, for instance take! In the warm weather we had last year, Silvia
and I would lose ourselves. We dined-out. We often dined
out. The conversation and laughter, the clink of silver-
ware; the birthdays we celebrated (hers and mines coming
on the heels of each other); Silvia's dresses, the perfume
she wore, I recall vividly still! At local restaurants, man-
agement loved and welcomed us. We remained often late
with the wine. Enchanted by the dreamlike weather, our
eyes were on occasions with unusual occurrences blessed,
beautiful things. Red! Yes, I remember. I remember red.
A drink one night spilled, patterning the black-and-white
checkered-floor unruly red; the liquid coagulated quickly,
with the together-drawn beads not staining the tiles, but
refilling the shattered receptacle (reassembled, and as if by
some conjuror's magic, again airborne), its contents undisturbed, upwards transported, back towards the table from
which it fell. I'm seeing it all again: my hand resting on
the cloth, the fabric of my sleeve the white cuffs, the styl-
ized lion-head pressed-on discs-of-gold links (a present
from Silvia), brightly glowing still, despite the subdued
lighting, and shadowed shifting overhead fronds; the crystal vessel half-empty now at rest, where moments before it
stood, as if nothing had happened! And—and indeed nothing had! Well. . .something did happen, something happened, yes, but it was nothing: it was a spoon that fell, the

waiter, down on one knee, discovers; the spilled drink and wine-stained tiles possibly of another night. No. I stand corrected. I stand corrected here—it was a spoon, not a glass, but a spoon from the set-up for an adjoining party, by a passing patron accidentally dislodged. With one from his pocket, the waiter replaced it, before returning to his station; there standing now, impregnable and solemn, replica almost of the oil-painting on the wall behind him, a period-piece depicting a man-servant, or some such person in attend of his charge. Magical those nights were! Magical. Silvia and I would, Silvia and I would—I'm sorry! I'm sorry! No. No, pardon me! Pardon me! I didn't. I didn't! I didn't get your previous statement—no! No. Yes. Maybe. No. Now please don't attach any unreasonable significance to the fact that my thoughts did for a minute or so wander! Please don't! Yes! No! I can explain! Let me explain! Please let me explain! I realized suddenly that I had neglected to attend to a duty of some importance. Reviewing this in my mind, my attention might have wavered somewhat; I missed part of your previous statement, yes. I don't think I'm not an alcoholic! No! That's not what I meant to say! I don't think I am—I mean I'm not an alcoholic! I did not swiftly respond to your questioning, that's true. But that doesn't make me an *anything!* It illustrates simply that I am incapable of doing two things at the same time. But I'm not in need of help—not yours, not the next person's, professional or otherwise—to deal with my 'problem', as everyone seems so keen in describing it these days!

O.K! Hold-up! Let's clarify something here! I'm not behind the wheel of a vehicle that's in motion. I'm not urinating in public. I'm not making a nuisance of myself. I fail to see why my blood/alcohol level should be of relevance. I mean—I mean if even I had been drinking heavily (and I've more or less admitted as much); presently was the worse for wine, and, thinking myself *Scarpia,* decided my version of, *E Lucevan Le Stelle* now to render (was at this moment, already loudly as my lungs permitted, so doing, let's say); as long as I held a key, and maintained reasonable pleasantness of voice, I don't see how anyone could be negatively impacted! Not too long ago, didn't a celebratory crowd roam this very land, amid shouts of, *Let's go Yanks!* Pretty loud they must have been, I have no doubt. Surely they urinated in public; if not now, certainly in times past, at least upon the corpses of the native redmen—did so ceremoniously hilariously blatantly too, I imagine! Has anyone since complained? Your phones haven't been ringing off the hooks, have they? I'm sure that the higher-ups at the local out-post broke not a sweat. No! I'm not trying to tell you how to do your job! I'm not! All I'm saying is, that skipping the bollocks and fuss, we could have directly gone to the *viand sale* of the matter, by simply visiting the Journal that is standard for 'usual suspects.' We call it JUSTUS, or something like that don't we! I'm listed therein I'm sure—along with the countless others, to which you may, when it suits your purpose, ascribe any one (or combination of) the innumerable offenses: murder in the senate, international terrorism, overt racism, disturbing the peace, bestiality, the stringing-up or burning alive of blacks in the wrong state in the wrong century and political climate; violating the double yellow-line on public roadways, necrophilia, distributing weapons without a permit; on certain individuals, in certain places, at certain times, an undesirable dress-code, color, scarf, or tie, God knows what else, conflicting with your non-ending catalog of unacceptable behavior; violated any single one of which would clear the way for apprehending, executing even (in broad daylight on a public street) an individual whose behavior, (or, in-the-future-far intended behavior), you imagined would be errant.

You gotta big mouth! You gotta big mouth! You don't know when to shut-up ! You gotta gotta big mouth . . .

Don't make me laugh! My mouth would get me into
trouble, you say. Don't you think I know that! I know that!
Every time you cradle an automatic weapon, twirl a pair
of handcuffs, or display any kind of restraining device —
or mention even of freedom of speech, I'm reminded!
Anyway, I'm always in trouble! I was born, you might
say into a world of trouble; even that, I screaming and
kicking, spewed out of what amounted to a whorl that was
trouble, you might say. And while no star in the east or
west heralded my arrival, that you would be unaware of
the overall confusion, the excruciating labor, the muci-
lage and mess, the textural weave of the filthy rags — the
bludklat even — that preceded, that were the banners, so to
speak, of my birth — is unlikely. Your files are frequently
updated, are they not! As *super*-power, you every day, tout
yourself, don't you! Hey! Anywhere in the world, if anyone should pick-up even a *shekere* or rattle a gourd of any
kind, anywhere — anywhere in the world, I hear tell — one
of your blokes somewhere in some way has immediate
knowledge of the intensity with which it shook, its deci-
bel-count and duration; and, before the last bead comes
to rest within its shell, is contemplating already by whose
authority and with what purpose it was, in the first place,
disturbed! Yet you question me, you question me, of a
night-time incidents in a part of the world you knocked-
off centuries ago, and lock, stock and barrel now own!
Roll back the tape! Let me see if I'm getting this right!
Someone called in a complaint! I 'match' the description.
I 'fit' the profile. You're doing a routine *confront and ob-
struct, interrupt and interpret, intern and interrogate, frisk
and whisk, slash and burn, romp and stomp, bunk and
dunk, massacre and land-grab* — or however else it is these
days officially regarded. You would never have bothered,
you would not have left your home, that all would have
been right with the world, you would have preferred! Relaxed, content and unassuming, you at present moment

most likely would have been ingesting of a cherry-pie while watching a western or a baseball game on television. Likkle Injans! Shagged your portly wife, you would be by now waking of a dreamless sleep, readying yourself for Sunday attendance before an effigy attached to a cross in a house of worship. What stories you sell! What movie magic they would make! Nine *Likkle Injans!* How neatly nansed your narratives! Hey man, all I'm trying to say is, had we engaged in none more than a form of silent-barter, exchanged hardly a word, shared not a single glance, you still could have done whatever it was you from the get-go intended to do. It would certainly have been, less painful (far as I am concerned, an easier pill to swallow, a less penetrating shaft to endure!) Look! You know something! Since we're telling stories that neither of us take seriously here, I think I might be able to come up with one of my own. Allow me! Allow me, please! Not long ago on the other side of the pond in what you would refer to as 'the old country', I happened to be. On a nighttime street, more out of boredom than anything else, I entered into contract with an old woman (her being toothless, plus the fact that she was easily affordable going not unnoticed, admittedly); for a certain service I paid—you, you know what I mean! Well, service you could say was rendered, just not satisfactorily so—if you get my drift. We disputed! I turned around—the old bag was gone! Thinking about it upsets me still! What I'm trying to say is: your grandmother owes me a buck or two! Your grandma—WHOA! LIGHTEN-UP! HEY! HEY! WHOA! TAKE IT EASY! WHAT'S THE MATTER WITH YOU! I WAS ONLY KIDDING, MAN! You know I was only kidding! That *hurt!* THAT HURT, MAN! You didn't have to do that! Alright! Alright! Alright! Alright! Sometimes I behave like I'm crazy! Sometimes maybe I am crazy! But that don't mean that you had to act the way you did! First of all, you don't need no Goddamn ID to tell you who I am! Let's cut the bull! You don't need ID any more than I need your pretending to be concerned about my well-being. We both know where we stand on that one! You know good and well who I am—good and well! Times were tough. Times were tough—remember? You needed to tote a heavy bale—I was there! Years later, there was a lull in criminal activity. Someone had goofed. New jailhouses were being completed more quickly than had been anticipated. Your superiors were on your backs like drugged-out pimps. You had a quota of collars to meet. I picked-up the slack! I and others like myself filled the half-empty court-houses. I read the scripts that were handed me. I did as I was told. I took my lumps. I never complained. Now I might know of, might even be *cause of,* some sort of disturbance on a night-time street, you say! I know of no disturbance! That night, *this night,* is night as any other, I only know! And as any other night, it disturbs *me,* it disturbs me still! That's all I know! By your own rankled heart, your nights might be troubled; with the asphalt of your dreams making it poisonous more perhaps! I gave. At the off, I gave! I did as I was told. All my life, I did as I was told! I'm paying dues still! My eldest is overseas right now fighting in the service; my son who, in my arms cried, only yesterday it seems still, when animals in the stories I read him died— my son, my flesh and blood, conditioned now not only to risk his own, but that he must weigh the lives even of strangers and their offspring, in countries which, up until now, he and I had never even heard of! You programmed him! You sent him there! You would never have been so bold! You would never have been so bold, if you didn't know who I was (how I came to be), who I am now, and that I fathered him! You don't need no ID—not for me, not for anyone else on this planet! And you didn't have to do what you just did! You didn't have to! But then again, what am I thinking! Wasn't that only you being yourself, the you you've always been! How long have you been get-

ting away with doing as you please! Why would you all
of a sudden need an ID—or reason even—to do as you've
forever done! You might even be within your rights—your
legal rights, I mean. For some peculiar reason, when it
comes to *legal rights,* like a cat, you seem always favorably on your feet to land. And it is late! You're right! I
should be off the streets. I'm sorry! I'm sorry I have a big
mouth, Sarge! Next time I'll watch what I say. I'll watch
my mouth, I promise. You're right! I'll get off the streets.
Don't worry about me. I'll fall in line one day. My injuries
offset now but my demeanor; they're not life-threatening.
And you're saying I'm free to go! Why should I be upset!
I'm not being detained or anything, am I? Hey, man! What
can I tell you! What can I say! What can I—Oh shit! You
know what! All this time I didn't realize that your partner
was a 'brother', just like me (he being in the shadows,
the tricky lighting and whatnot). Just like me! Ain't that
a bitch! I mean, I'm just like him! I mean! I mean! Hey,
look after yourself, man! Look after yourself, eh Sarge!
You and your partner, look after yourselves! Mikky-Fik-
ky! Howd'ya like that! *A brother!* An *American-African!*
I mean an *African-American!* I mean, I mean—you know
what I mean! A *Blokemons!* Hey, look after yourselves,
fellas! Look after yourselves eh! Goodnight! Goodnight,
Sarge! *Brother!* Goodnight Sarge. Sarge.

    That encounter didn't really take place—no it didn't!
That was me, only (I think) me, rambling as usual, inside
my own head—well, me, Mr. Hennessy, and a few other
kindred spirits, that is! Far as I know, I've never been in
the service, and my only son is not in the military. I'm not
the forever-victim, nor the injured-most soul I portray myself regularly to be. I've had my share of hard knocks, yes,
but I usually slip most of the punches that come my way;
responded on occasions more than once with jabs of me
own—started shit sometimes too, truth be told! Still, the
threats I'm beginning lately to feel might not all be imagi-

nary. More than a few times, I found myself in trouble because of my ill-functioning memory. I should remember to remain mainly silent. Being a big-mouth is not good, but then so sometimes is not speaking-up for your rights. Not everyone buys my stories. One of these days, I may be called upon to give substantive accounts of my current and past activities. How am I going to do that, when sometimes I have a problem remembering even my own name! God, where would I start! The doggas did show-up, though! I damn sure didn't imagine that part of the story! They showed-up alright. The patrol-car cruised alongside me for about half a block. I ignored them. Suddenly, with their siren blaring and lights flashing, they sped away. I don't like these close calls. The next time, I might not be so lucky. It's quite a stretch of the imagination from *Il Doumo di Pisa* in Italy, to the streets of Hoboken—quite a stretch! Still, the uncertainty and apprehensiveness of the days immediately following the business with Silvia, have begun lately to harrow me again (and, with it, the disorientation, memory loss, and, God knows, what else). Boy, how different things are now from the day—has it already been six months—I first arrived in Hoboken, vowing secretly that I would blend in, and make myself indistinguishable from those around me! Now I'm probably one of the shelter's more noticeable residents. Just recently, a rather smartly-attired, not at all unattractive I initially thought, middle-aged woman approached me, as I waited for the lights to change, at one of the intersections on Washington Street; saying as she offered her hand, something in Italian which sounded like, 'Hello, my friend! How goes things!' I'd never laid eyes on this person before! Set-up, I immediately thought! Set-up! Hers was the affected casualness of someone briefed by the authorities. She was bait! Undercover were everywhere! Any minute now they were going to slip a pair of handcuffs on me! It was only after being almost run-over by a delivery truck, as with the eyes and expression no doubt, of someone gone suddenly mad, I had bolted across the street, almost toppling a cart of groceries onto a stroller in which at his petrified mother's feet a tiny infant slept, that I came to my senses. The poor woman was still standing, on the other side of the street where I left her, stunned out of her wits, with a puzzled expression on her face: the proprietress of a small clothing store a little further along the block she was! Throughout the summer, it had been ritual that I would on my morning walk, visit with her (she befriended me, I think it was, on my second or third day in Hoboken), to sit and chat, on occasion to enjoy even coffee and some of the delightful pastry she seemed always to have on hand. (When she was young she lived for a brief period close to Renata Tebaldi; knew the young soprano, and of herself dreamed even once, as having a career in musical theater. Some of the flamboyance of the stage must reside within her still. She had, since I'd seen her last, dramatically altered the color of her hair).

How unscripted, these performances—how unpredictable! This wasn't the first such incident. Where began this deformity of the brain! The inability to accurately recall, when did it start? Where-from came, this march without end! Sometimes I imagine a sea, the far side of a river or great lake. Sometimes, I remember a hill that sloped (of a particular day, remember the trees there dancing in the wind); but with what purpose? How much of a distance in space and time, by what manner craft, over which type track of land or body of water, was I, from my point of departure, wherever that was, towards this untidy mess transported! When did all this begin? There must have been a beginning! Everything has its beginning, this earth, this life, the great mill of stars in the sky; the coward's dream of an empire, everything! Everything begins. Even of heaven and hell, we know that Lucifer's falling-out with God paved the way for the lower province. Yet as to the commencement of my own now seemingly unending flight, at a loss I remain still. As to precisely where I came from, I remember nothing. Maybe I was programmed to remember nothing! Maybe I am nothing. Maybe I am zero. Maybe my zero brain underwent some form of conditioning, a mucking-around with even of its zero content, a blanking further even of its empty screen. I sometimes recall (no doubt of late-night run-ins with the doggas) the back of a hand on more than one occasion across my face; a blow to the stomach that caused me to vomit, a voice repeatedly screaming, *'Don't lie to me!'* I couldn't be imagining all of these things! Perhaps more viciously stringently within the unacknowledged 'black-hole' of a secret prison in a foreign country, my 'briefing', 'interrogation', 'softening-up', or whatever it was, took place! There must be good reason why I often in my mind's eye see, as if frozen in a dream, an image of myself shackled to a chair, a hooded figure with a dog by his side, standing close, his arm raised, his fingers into a fist curled that he would in a moment strike! No. He's not going to! He hasn't struck! As of now he hasn't. (I would be feeling the pain still.) But that he didn't earlier-on, I'm not sure. A drug might have been administered. Yes, a drug. Yes. No, I can't be sure. I can't be sure of anything right now. An off-and-on whirring like that of a dental-drill (somewhat muffled), coming from not too far away, I'm hearing now! I'm hearing it again . . . someone moaning; a churning too, of liquid, coming from one of the dark alcoves in a wall. The silence prolonged, ended; ended how long ago now, whether hours, days or weeks, whether yet to begin, I am imagining it from a previous like-encounter, I am unable still to tell. None the worse I am for wear, I don't think. Of physical scares, I'm in possession not of any—far as I can tell, I'm not. I have no doubt though, that wherever it was, whenever it was, I agreed, to some form of what they call a, *No lo contendere,* to the charges my captors were (mother's iron-lung U-bet) holding over my head. Anyway, even if I didn't then, and only imagined that I did, I do so now! God, if only to get the medical attention I obviously need, I'll sign anything; do whatever is asked of me, whatever is asked of me I will do. I—I, Rotschild Jarvis, having from the horizontal to the hypotenuse rose, perpendicular now, and being of mind and body (far as I know, mind and body) sound, willingly agree, willingly agree to furthermore, to further . . . more, more to further—I'll NOT agree! What I'm I saying! I don't agree! I'll not agree to anything furthermore, that's what! I won't agree! No! No! No, I say! I won't! It doesn't matter! It doesn't matter what I said! It doesn't matter what I said before, whether a moment ago, or an eternity ago—I've changed my mind! I'm allowed to do that, am I not? Well I did! I don't agree! I don't recall! I have no recollection. I can't one way or the other determine! I can't say! Don't know! Don't know! Not sure! What? What was the question? I don't understand the question! Eh? Eh? Yes. No. No. No. Yes. Yes. No. No. Yes. I don't feel well! I don't know nothing! *I can't breathe! I can't breathe! Oh God! I can't breathe! Please let me breathe! Please let me breathe! Why won't you let me breathe!* I don't know nothing, I tell you! I don't know nothing! I'm not in a position to say! I won't agree! There are rules governing this sort of thing! A lawyer should be present! I should have a lawyer! A witness! I need a witness! Someone! Anyone! I don't agree! I don't agree! I don't, I don't! I don't, period, that is *period*. Period.

There are no fresh needle marks on my arm. I wasn't injected with anything. Let's put these kinds of thought behind us. I'm still in one piece. Now, as to what happened earlier tonight, let's say that the mix-up with the drinks, the mix-up even with the mix-up in itself, whether cognac, brandy, champagne, or non-sparkling wine, whatever whichever however; whether a single drink, whether

all the drinks, had been paid for—had not been paid for;
the question of who ordered what and when, who should
have received it, and didn't; who should not have, and
did—had all been staged, earlier in the day, the drug-deal-
er, but a 'plant', an undercover, a who-knows-what agent
of the State, a veteran of the armed-services, or active-still
member of one of those quasi-military units, guaranteed
immunity for his crimes, the murder (or, if you prefer, 'ac-
cidental death') of an innocent civilian (or civilians); elsewhere happened, but not yet brought to light, even uncom-
mitted still, yet no doubt soon will be, probably (usually)
in, another country, some day, under circumstances which
would make it not easy to relegate blame, or even to determine if anything occurred in the first place (the kind of
scenario we every day without thinking face). The dealer
was not a dealer! O.K. That would account for his near-
mechanical clumsiness! A dealer would not have been so
matter-of-fact; he would have had one eye on the street,
while at least attempting with the other, to interpret the
nuances of expression on the faces of the towards-him forever advancing line of desperate individuals, with money
in their hands, a junkie's hunger in their eyes. Some grimace or twitch or stance, unusual apparel, omen of the
street, whatever—might help him to determine whether
(with back-up near) one of them carried under his shirt, a
badge attached to a chain around his neck, and a weapon
he was anxious to use, concealed on his person somewhere (only in this case, it was—it might, it could have
been, the 'dealer' himself that was *cover);* strategy being
for whatever reasons: to afford the intended quarry access
to the bait, to allow rather than prevail upon him (me/you/
whomever) from retrieving it, the purpose: tag, rather than
ensnare; or, to use the parlance, *observe but not detain;*
a tactic the *kanigianni* sometimes employ, regarding individuals under surveillance for 'serious' offenses. The
suspect (me/you/whoever) reckless, of course, continues

complacent as before, non-aware, non-more cautious, the-wiser-non, except . . . except when you get the feeling, that feeling, you know, that now-and-again feeling that always gets the better of you. In the past, you've had it often. Lately you've been getting it more and more. You scored. You scored some dope! Someone's behind you. Turn the corner—quick! You turn the corner! Someone's behind you! Someone's behind you still. This way! Cut through the park! Through the park, yes! No! No—exit! Exit! You trapped! You're trapped in the viewfinder of someone's camera, with others insect-like and fleeing you're trapped! Someone's recording you. Someone's camera is recording your every move. You scored. You scored dope! Some-one's following you. Someone followed you into the park. You're—nauseous? Look! Behind you look! Interrupt-ing his strides, as if to gather of something (or someone) advancing upon him from the rear, a dressed-in-battle-fatigues vague gaunt figure his own head turns, seem to gesture at you mockingly, a blur of whirring confetti be-comes; before merging into the sudden dark ensemble of dense-leafed trees near a shaded area wherein, quickly, amid flecks of sunlight, he disappears . . .

Now, that's not thunder! Those are not horses hooves! A clink of armor? No! No, those are rats atop the mounds of garbage! That's only the wind disturbing the cans amid the debris. There was no frail girl once underage, nor within earshot recent of a passer's-by demented designs violated; no ears turned deaf to her cries, no eyes that even though morning was light, saw yet none, not even the ethnicity of the assailant (nor that he was different, dif-ferent from themselves; a vagrant, the usual suspect type, he!) He! It must be he! It was he! He this moment down a lonely street, on a lonely night, in a lonely city, that walks; the townsfolk hardly abuzz, the media silent (advisedly so?) the horrifying details, not on everyone lips; no se-cret gathering of families and clans vowing to avenge the wrongs befallen their people and country, their kith and kin, their heart and homeland; swearing no oath in blood to oust not even the strangers in their midst; no posse of men, no torches in the night, no horses at gallop. Those were rats in their scurried flight, overturning the cans in the debris, rats, rats you say! Rats eh! Those were no rats. No rats, my friend! I good and long in the woodpile hid! I know to distinguish from others non-threatening and benign, the sound of hobnails on the cobblestones; the thunder with their hooves that horses make, when under the cover of night, they gallop in the dust! I recognize the villain in apparel rewoven, the swathed-in-bandages victim, the feigned injuries, the fake blood. These images in my memory still live, the adjusted face-mask, the scabbard carefully hidden, the secret tally sheet—

Look! There's someone out there! There's someone out there! Someone's out there, I tell you! Where'd he go! Where'd he go! He'd better not come near me! You see this shank! You see this shank in my hand! He'd better not come near me! Where'd he go!

Come on! We don't want none o' that! We don't want none o' that, now! O.K? None o' that! Calm down! There's nothing out there! Calm down! You know what that shit does to your brain! You're off to the races again. Silvia was right. You ought to stop messing with the stuff! You've been your own worst enemy for too long! You don't own a shank! You don't possess any kind of weapon, but the plastic knife with which you butter your toast each morning—and even that, you don't own! Even a quill you don't have, not even a quill with which to scratch even the journal filthy, dog-eared and frayed, of which, in your hands near still blank, you say, you always say God willing one day you'll write. One day! One day! One day! There's nothing out there! Nothing out there, I tell you!

Chill! Chill for a minute! Calm yourself! Let's use our loaves! Let's get clever! Let's wake-up, and at the same time play lifeless, so that we see who's quick to sniff-out the rot of carcasses, who with the tallying of each cadaver, quietly smiles; who most efficiently produces the body-bags—who most expeditiously fills them! Let's see who wanders the garbage-dumps late at night, whose shit is stashed in the debris, who tends the secret cemeteries! It is midnight, isn't it! Let's invoke a few spirits of our own. We hold ourselves in too good stead for this kind of nonsense—in too good stead. Just calm down! Of other things (or, if of the same, at least, in different ways), let's together review! Let's knock heads. And if even only for moments brief, let's hand in hand, with silence, walk . . .

O. K! Of the night, of the night in question, of the drinks, shall we say—since they might be the cause of the present uncertainty and confusion. Let's of the drinks say, yes! That one was intended, not for yourself, but for someone else, let's say! Isn't this a possibility, always! Cases of mistakenly-targeted victims, individuals being in the wrong place at the wrong time, are rampant nowadays, are they not? Isn't 'collateral damage', as they call it, the inescapable *humansplatt* (alright, *bugsplatt,* if you like) part & parcel of our times! Getting hit by a stray bullet (often with 'adverse' effects), is commonplace, is it not? Anyone who reads the newspapers or watches television, can't but notice the frequency of the kill-offs, and must (we might by their reticence assume) of the carnage, the targeting of two or three (sometimes even an entire village) to get one, quietly approve! Perhaps we are all of us in the same crossfire caught. Who knows! O.K! A glass half-filled sat in front of me. I drank of it. Things like that happen. I saw a movie once, where the good-guy accidentally downed a drink that was laced with a lethal substance. That was a movie, good-guy/bad-guy stuff, fiction, someone's imagination. This, unfortunately, is real, here and now real; real

as a Sunday real; real as a kid being blown off his bicycle
on the street outside his grandmother's home, real; as, on
the other side of the world, the limbs with blood not-yet
dried of a civilian family remain scattered in the dust at the
foot of a mountain, the mistaken target of a for-good-rea-
son, this-that-or-the-other strike, of which we know not
much, of which we never know much, except that it in-
volves metal and heat, that it travels fast, and that it sears
human flesh—real. By occurrences such as these (the daily dead), our clocks could easily be set nowadays! Alright.
Alright then! It is between mid-night and dawn, judging
from where we presently are; and, regarding the spherical
mass of earth beneath our feet, I would say, in a city on the
half upper-more of the continent of Amerika. In astronom-
ical terms, I guess that's precise enough. You'd want me to
be more particular, I know! O.K! We're in Hoboken—
Hoboken, New Jersey. Earlier on, there was doubt, admittedly, as to whether we were looking out over the River
Hudson, or from Corsica at the Tyhrrenian Sea. That question has been put to rest. Everyone concedes that there are
two sides to the Atlantic, Amerika (the continent of) centuries ago discovered—proclaimed. Confusion! Gunfire.
A few people died! Alright, a lot of the local people died!
Alright. a great majority—O. KAY! O Kay. They were
massacred. There are documents, dates, monuments, com-
memorative works. Places: Delaware; men: Washington,
Hamilton coming out of the Antillian Archipelago, others;
there are numbers: ten nine eight seven six one—correct?
Not quite! Seven six five four, scores-years and three two
zero (one)? Lunes! Martes! Mercury! Brain functioning,
brain functioning still! No problem. Pulse, steady: X
heartbeats per minute? X heartbeats per. Walk a straight
line. O.K. No. No redman nor cowboy good-guy/bad-guy
stuff, at least none more so than in any other milieu anywhere else on the face of the globe: no evidence still, none
whatever of a drink being tampered with, or being con-

taminated in any way (not here, not anywhere). Another possibility! Simpler explanation: the earlier nausea, severe though it might have been, the headache which caused me to pass out (how long for, I don't know; I can't remember still) could have been the result of something I ate, or of other substances, which during the last few days (not to mention the last few years), I put into my system, voluntarily. Maybe no one is to blame. Maybe no one bashed me on the head. Maybe in a drunken stupor, I fell. Perhaps a sometimes unusual taste of mouth, occasional light-headiness, a fainting spell, blurred vision (along with, the now-and-again erectile dysfunction) might be normal for a man of my age. The notes in Dr. Zimmerman's office—even with his dramatic reaction, even with the blacked-out lines and paragraphs, could have been just that: *notes*—no more, no less. The shelter offers a once-a-week class on creative writing. (I sat in a couple of times.) One of the attendees could have authored those pages. They were a loony enough bunch (myself, perhaps not the least among them, some might argue). The case histories were, from the little I remember, far-fetched, off-the-wall: mind-altering chemicals surreptitiously administered, diabolical scientists, deranged mutants; zombie-robots roaming the streets, believing that they are not just one but two selves; forever expecting of the rain; some not recognizing their own reflected images in the mirror. Bugged-out lunacy! Space-shit! Fiction! Who knows! I talk to myself. I 'see things!' Maybe I'm the one that's zoned. Perhaps my theories don't amount to anything. The name of the movie was *D. O. A.* I remember now, yes, 'Dead-On-Arrival.' Beginning: The lead-character realizing that he had been poisoned, enters a station-house, weak, but under his own steam; he tells his story; we listen-in: a convoluted tale, he dies. Finis. The movie ends. Silvia and I leave the theater—no: by myself I walked! I was by myself. I re-

member I was by myself that night, yes. Someone followed me all the way. Clever he was too, his feet silent,
never making a sound; in the shadows he remained, close
always to the wall. Once or twice he might have coughed,
or cleared his throat (deliberately perhaps, to let me know
that he was there), I'm not sure. I'm not sure of anything.
Maybe it wasn't he who coughed. Maybe it was an inadvertent passer-by. Maybe he wasn't following me. Who
knows! Maybe I was never followed. What if I were never
followed—not on that night, not last night, nor on any of
the previous ones! What if even the sounds I hear as I walk
the late-hours darkened streets are none but my own; that
in my current skewed state of mind, I'm incapable often
even of separating, the sounds made by the hard soles of
my shoes as they collide, one after the other, with the sidewalk, but in addition to, and juxtapose with them, hear
miscellaneous others coming out of the clouded ill-functioning data-bank of my memory, reverberating faintly
still, the embellished remnants of a jumble of percussive
choruses, the frantic feet of endless commuters, hurrying
first this way, then that way; stopping short sometimes,
starting again—pirouetting; dashing-off in various direction, barely making their connections, barely missing their
connections; a daily ritual, the troubled toccata to a frenzied dance on the polished floors of train stations during
rush-hours in large cities (the large cities, all the large cities I over the years traversed, and nightly now in the torment of my dreams, re-visit); a curtain of discarded fragmented sounds, clanks, whistles, cries, *rara rara;*
collective voices, hisses, shouts, departing trains, over-
heard fragments of conversations, miscellaneous distorted
brief sentences, half-syllables, of words, echoing inside
me: *rara rara, rara rara!* What if there was no D.O.A.
stamp and pad on the desk in front of no sergeant goofing
around with fellow-doggas, not expecting me to, upon entering the station-house, babble incoherent, incomprehen-

sible syllables, in quick time only to gasp and double-over, mouth agape, eyes unseeing, grotesque and motionless in a instant gargoyle-like *rigor mortis* at their feet, on the ground, before them! On the other hand, let's say that I never arrived, of my absence, none did notice take; there was no movie in the works chronicling my days, no telling of anecdotes, no group of in-the-morning men, remembering fondly sadly briefly, their once-was colleague (deceased, they'd assume, perhaps now), of whom they might imagine, sipping with them invisibly, coffee; breaking bread, early briefly; as another day unfolds, sharing again, a joke and a laugh; a collage of dreams, remembrance of things how they were, how they could have been, whether they might be, whether they might have been, had they, had they not, one way or the other, in the first place! Oh, that I would be he, he/him, any he, any him, on any street, in any city on any given day, at any given time of day; under whatever circumstance; and remain, not as I have been these years long in life's *lapsap,* among its 'usual suspects', its unusual suspects, its army of disparates and miscreants and misfits, stood; living, at the same time, in a shelter, doing well in Europe, driving an expensive *macchina,* residing at prestigious addresses; on the run, wanted for questioning on matters trivial and minor; of no visible means of support, no fixed abode, sleeping on the stairwells of buildings in the city; knowing something of nothing, knowing nothing of something; going weeks on end without a bath or change of clothing; dressed in turned-to-rags hand-me-downs; wearing custom-made suits, Zimerly underwear, hand-made shoes; being involved, not being involved in the suspicious drowning, the perhaps murder of a wealthy socialite; a non-credible/incredible, a what-have-you/whatever, apprehended however/wherever to be; non-visible, non-discernible, obscured by a backdrop of souls to myself God alone knows how many similar, amid the clutter and cluster, the clamor and the chaos of cities and ideas, and stats and crimes and things; non-visibly, unimaginably, irretrievably, beyond-redemption wedged between the odd and even numbers, close to the zeroes and the ones, amid persons 'of interest', wanted-dead-or-alive with wounds that are, though bleeding profusely, non life-threatening yet still; unnoticed again amid the painful restrictive-devices, the sledge-hammers and chains and lashes and rocks and stones.

You're right! Once again, I must admit, you're right! I should move on. I would only make myself ill. I would only make myself ill again. There are no sinister plots, none known to everyone but myself, no secret dossiers; no one is planning to have me murdered, any more than to, in a grand conspiracy, pretend with others that I don't exist—that I never existed! True, more and more sophisticated memory-scrambling devices are being developed every day—but that the agencies which supervise, and control them (and guard them jealously, let's not forget), would have had a hand in my overall confusion of mind, is more than unlikely. Come on! There were no shredding of documents. There could not have been! To yourself relevant, there were none, in the first place (at least, I don't think so). Let's be real! No-one either way cares. I'm not running for office, nor would I even if, of crimes, the national out-put was dramatically increased, the caliber of criminals, the definition for criminality altered, down-graded a thousand-fold) be candidate for any list of individuals wanted by the authorities. Mine would be a kill/capture, entirely without merit (laughable almost); without beneficiaries, or benefit of any kind. My anonymous ordinariness, quiet as it's kept, might (should) even qualify me for some kind of exemption! By the same token, as to whether I breathe the air or not, a no-ask/no-tell policy, among the minds that concern themselves with such matters, perhaps more likely suffices, anyway. There is no plot whatsoever, none nowhere; nowhere in the world, none; none, except the ones which I like purposeless edifices create with the incomplete erecto-set of a deranged mind, none other than the ones I assemble; and, before they crumble to the ground, disassemble and readily re-assemble, creating absurdities, anomalies, falsehoods, contradictions, deceptive facades, miscellaneous props and scenery, purposeless escarpments, frightful monstrosities, in the theater of my brain; artifacts forged in the misshapen rotunda of a remote kingdom, amid the shadows beneath the dome of my skull! What if it were only I—I and I alone, together with myself, my other selves; I, scenarist/audience director/actor hero/villain innocent by-stander, playing all the roles, roaming the streets, panhandling, boosting, accepting handouts, groping women; selling drugs, being my own best costumer, using my own stuff; selling my script; poisoning minds, poisoning my own beverages, delivering pizzas, reading notes from top-secret files, hacking into, and downloading documents from classified web-sites, causing mayhem, a favorite of the mediarists, the meat of biographers, hanging-out at a celebrated luncheonette in the city, breakfasting with high-finance blokes, calling them by their first names, pretending that I too was of substance, and that I had a career and a family to go home to; comfortable with whites, at home amongst the new black-ristos, ha-ha-ha-ha-ha-ing and kiki-ing with them on morning talk-shows, wearing a suit and tie, enjoying celebrity-ship; acquiring an entourage, my face and smile, a banner for the future; walking around with life-sized photographs and effigies of myself, affecting an incomprehensible jargon, an arrogant curious stridulant non-human tone of voice, *quaqua quaquaquaquaquaqua;* running for office, a candidate for the presidency, *quaqua quaquaquaquaquaqua;* presidential as a candidate *quaqua quaquaquaquaquaqua;* becoming first a hit, then a hit-man; winning, winning the presidency, *quaqua quaquaquaquaquaqua;* being inaugurated, taking an oath of office: I, *quaqua quaquaquaquaquaqua,* do solemnly *quaqua quaquaquaqua;* do solemnly, do solemnly *quaqua quaquaquaquaqua* whatever; inducted into a hallowed hall, winning a prize for peace; saving the world, destroying the world, accusing myself (accusing total strangers, even fictitious, non-existent individuals) of heinous crimes that might (that, in all likelihood, might not) have been committed; proclaiming my innocence of others, which because of my self-induced amnesia, I might quite easily have committed and now *quaqua quaquaquaquaqua* no recollection of them; none, *quaqua quaquaqua; quaqua quaquaqua* whatsoever *quaquaquaquaqua quaquaquaquaquaquaqua quaquaquaquaquaquaquaqua* have!

To think absolutely nothing, to nail shut the windows of the mind, even for a few seconds, is unimaginable. A man without eyes sees still; he sees because he must, be it but the one and only color, the single hue reflecting the unchanging degree (or absence even) of light, he and he alone blindly sees as long as he blindly lives. He sees because he thinks, he thinks because he lives; and to live and not think (or have the mind set blank, it's monitor at zero, or zero-think) is not possible. The comatose even, must be aware of that odd (however brief and faint) glimmer which from time to time would penetrate his encapsulated world. There might be a mystic (in Himalya somewhere perhaps) who could near-empty himself of all images and thought; but that it would not have taken strict discipline and a number of years for him to do so, not many would argue. All I know is that the more I think the more I think the more I think! That it still is dark, I think; the air is fresh, rain falls; with the noonday sun directly overhead, silhouettes at my feet a rabble dance, I think! Even as I think I think; the earth rotates, and as the sun nears the horizon, shadows lengthen, they lengthen and multiply; they multiply until all is dark, until all is shadow; and everything everywhere is with darkness covered—everything but the

imagined light from a single shaft, the paltry fire of my
being, the dream in which, unnoticed among shadows I
exist; among shadows. yes, even among the shadows; a
shadow myself, unheeded and unheralded, I am! I think!
Look! I would be happy if I could avoid the tangents of
thought by which I'm plagued; if I could fill the gaps in my
memory; the periods during which I forget, except for occasional flashes and fragments, not only the reason (if there
is one) for my journey, but things as elementary as, the
purpose even of my being positioned on a city street, at a
particular time of day; whether in one direction or another,
I intended to advance, or for what reason stationary at an
intersection, I chose to remain. Why am I here, why now,
why on this corner, near the top of this hill, contemplating
how soon the sun will rise; has it risen already, whether it
sailed across the heavens, as yesterday it did; how dark it
was a few moments ago, how mild the flow of traffic, why
so quiet the dawn! Is the light now already broad, or are
my eyes gradually growing adjusted to, becoming more
and more comfortable with the dark, that I now at earlier
and earlier moments in time, imagine light coming from
the sun! Is it already within tomorrow's dream that I wander miserably aimlessly along the river-front! Is it already
tomorrow! A stranger will appear, a stranger always appears, a stranger with a dog at the end of a leash in his
hand, his arrival (without fail) a few moments after my
own. The dog flicks its ears, the man, leaning towards it,
whispers a command; the dog, sometimes in a human
voice (monosyllables usually) but more often with compli-
ance and timorous gesture, responds. For a while, the three
of us are motionless. Then, glancing neither one way nor
the other, I'll walk quietly down the hill. Before I get to the
water's edge, one of them, with purposefully distorted delivery, makes (intended for my ears, I have no doubt) a
disparaging remark (tone-of-voice alerts me) in a foreign
language, the stressed final-syllable reverberating intermi-

nably sometimes it seems. Following a yelp or cry from the canine, all sound is abated, the morning silent again, man and beast vanished, or to from whence they came, quietly returned; the silence ends, it is tomorrow, tomorrow again; near the same scenario reenacted, reenacted twenty-four hours from now, though by then I will have forgotten, forgotten until just before the sun begins its arc in the sky, sometimes even long after, what happened the day before; what happened yesterday, I will have forgotten; forgotten the man, forgotten his dog, forgotten even that yesterday was yesterday; that a young girl was savagely molested, someone was carjacked, someone was killed, Shah is relocated and lives in Brooklyn, the following day's (that is, today's) temperature unusually high; had I already done so, or should I now visit, the proprietress of a clothing store on one of the adjoining streets! I will have forgotten it all, the looming mayhem, the mushrooming morning, heralding for me, the same apprehensiveness, the same suspicion, the same bludgeoning fear, as on that very first day at the shelter, my arrival precisely where from, and with what circumstance, a mystery still! Yet I remember vividly clearly, a hill that sloped towards the water's edge. I remember it being, like this one, lined with trees leafed September-red and gold, the days yet warm, the stars at night by clouds obscured, in one of the villages along the Adriatic coast. And I seem to recall hearing word somewhere too, of a man living not far from it being stabbed to death, by a drifting stranger who didn't like dogs—or was it the man, a local merchant, who overpowered the wayfarer and killed his dog, using not a knife, but a gun to do so; then blamed it on his brother, so that he (the merchant) became first in line for some kind of family fortune! Sometimes I try to not think, to not think at all (even though, I know from having tried so many times before, that it is not possible to do so). Sometimes I wonder whether I am enmeshed in a net of dreams, my own net, cast by my own dreams, in the whirlpool of my own making! Whether even now I'm awake, or dreaming still, I'm not sure. There are things about ourselves, simple things that are, at the same time, difficult for us to understand, that are perhaps not meant for us to understand. Still we try, if only to understand a little more, we try; a little more of something—of anything, a something of something, as opposed to nothing of something, or nothing at all, we try to understand. Is it to understand, that I again find myself exploring a desolate frozen landscape, made by my exhausted eyes, desolate and frozen each time more, only to in the end purchase a few milligrams of crystalline substance from a stranger whose name I fail forever to remember, though even his dog, even from a distance, seems always to recognize me, flicking its ears and yelping, the moment I commence my ascent of the little hill atop which like Stuarts they remain; the master cordial and inexplicably more than generous at times, the beast licking my hands, begins to whine and cry the moment I start to retreat! Is it to know, to know something, that I snap the cover off the labeled-vials in my hand, only to re-attach them, without taking (refusing still to take) my prescribed medication? Is all this in some way related to Silvia demise! Is it with hopes that I would once more hear the rasp of her voice that I over and over walk down this hill! Did she and I once long ago walk down a hill similarly-sloped, the leaves there too rustling in the wind, the twigs snapping amid the gravel at our feet; with the sun on our faces warm, the laughing sound of children in the near-by playground ringing pleasantly always in our ears! These chains that link me to specific places, to people and things, I must break. There are certain threads of thoughts I must stifle. Right now Silvia might be deceased. She was a total stranger. I must not think of her in any other way! That I would never see her face again, should bother me none; nor should the circumstance of her death cause me concern. I have nothing to hide. With no one's blood am I sullied. I carry nowhere on my person, the stain of guilt! My conscience is clear! And if nothing, if nothing else, there is something I understand, something I've always understood—that I am without blame, I understand. No one blames me. With life's grind I would not be troubled; nor with its scathe, nor with its scabs; nor with the laboring of its passage, would I allow myself to be unnecessarily burdened! I should shrug my shoulders, I should shrug my shoulders and move on. I must defy the forces attempting to relegate me to this exile. From even the castle/prison of my skin, one day I will escape! I wrestle with my sanity now, but I still will try! If unsuccessful, I will try again! Every man, in his own way tries; every man his secret mountains to climb, winged-horses to ride, his animal hides to collect, the walls of a prison that restricts him to penetrate. Finding himself battered and bruised, fallen sometimes and afraid, he stands always again; even with his dream's last remnants, a star-distant pinpoint in the far, his mind's mirror with disarrayed images unhinged, he searches still; searches as all his life he has, that he may find that again which will make him fresh again, new again; that something, that anything, upon which he would hang his name, an I.O.U. he would cash, a Pantheon he would design; the ceiling of a chapel he would paint; his own pramantha he would be, fire he would steal from the gods, serum for immortality he would hold in his hands; a bridge beyond oblivion, standing upon which, he would survey, and from which, ultimately, he would himself be judged. Distinguish from others, he would take his place besides the icons in time! What if! What if all the trying were none! What if, in the final analysis I am nothing. What if, 1=0; what if, 0=1, and that the zeroes and ones, together with all the numbers, all the numbers in the world came up still to nothing—none, none whatsoever; none and none again, plus none; my lonely imagination, a buckled-wheel journey across the lopsided landscape of a dream, a dying dream, the dream of my death, the death and dream of all men, coming up short, being by an over-whelming force hurled onto the abrasive jagged rocks of an unyielding planet, running headfirst into the comet's-tail of bricks with which at some point we all collide, some more violently than others, some numbed by drugs—by drugs and the boogied raggedness of their lives—never see it coming, never feel its effects, shrug their shoulders, yes, even with bones broken, and limbs lacerated, they simply shrug their shoulders and move on; move on as if nothing, nothing at all, had happened; others not so fortunate. Am I losing my mind? Maybe we all are. Maybe everyone is mad. Maybe everyone is sane. Maybe I'm the one that's whack-o. Maybe I'm bugging. Maybe you can't win 'em all! Maybe you can't lose 'em all! Maybe rain must fall. Maybe it's going to pour. Maybe every dog will have it's day! Is this day mine! Is this day mine! I grasp the pen. I write! The letters take shape. Droplets of blood from the hardly-healed wounds in my side, in the palms of my hands, and from those caused by the thorns in my head, fall like asterisks of rain onto the pages, bright again, red again, red like blood, like blood again, blood, again . . .

V

People of Hoboken! Forgive a non-Christian Gulliver, whose odd brain, ravished by excesses, functions now but barely, amid the seeds of larceny and heart-lodged discontent, in bastion Christian America; a renegade Rawan with screws loose and wires crossed, clanking aimlessly onward, I did not rot but rested only on the streets of your city. People of Hoboken! Forgive me!

Take heart! Take heart, friend! All is not lost. Chin up! We began this journey together, we'll end it so. Base-camp is but a mind-set away, out-of-reach it never was. The problem is but a simple one; the solution might be equally so. Rotschild Jarvis (Locker No. 28) last night should have alcohol and drug-free dined and slumbered within the tolerably safe refuge anonymous individuals had out of their heart's kindness provided, so that he and others similarly-distressed would not during nighttime hours be roaming the streets of Hoboken. He should have directed his footsteps to the shelter for homeless persons at the lower-level of a church on Bloomfield Street, right here in the center of town. He should have carried himself through its portals, no later than (as is by staff requested) 10 P.M. He didn't. A death-penalty case? Not at all! A believable excuse could be had! (One is required, letting it be known ahead of time that the curfew deadline is to be missed.) One is required, yes; and, yes, one could always be manufactured! Salvation! I started off with good intent! *Happened!* I found myself thrown off stride by someone acting peculiarly inside a shop that sold ladies things. I altered course, choosing for safety's sake, a route more circuitous, (and, consequently, less expedient than those which were customary); to discover myself before I knew it, short of time. Realizing that it was—that it would have been—by then, of entry into the facility difficult, I gambled instead with the burden of night. I talked to myself, trying to straighten out my thinking as I walked. Walking by oneself usually is a kind of therapy, is it not? Yes! I walked the streets, accompanied by my thoughts all night . . . I could say that, yes! Yes, I could! But . . . this story, though true (true of sort) might still not, at the same time, I don't think, weigh much with shelter officialdom (of it, non-ending versions may have pounded already wearily upon their ear-drums). Whenever the temperature turns hospitable, as it has been these last days, it is not unusual for many a shelter resident to discover himself missing-in-action, dallying somewhere in the forays of his night—days we suffer, though the sun hardly sets sometimes, before we are ourselves of old again, delinquent again, unmindful again, indifferent again. Out of twilight, our fields of vision to narrow, our senses to merry make, spirits capricious almost singing appear! Night, of nature sweet, deceives us; gathers quick its shroud, takes flight; leaving a morrow of dreams. The day with its grimaces and sneers, gauge and weigh us; its disparates and discrepancies, its doubt and error, reminding us: this is you, this is you, this is you; wandering the predawn haze of an unfamiliar city, you; the morning twigs crackling beneath the damp foliage, the dimness of the the mist, you; the sun darting towards the zenith in braids of fire, you, you, you! The rest, your grand designs, your feeble excuses, your subterfuge, and schemes, be rid of! Put the chemical substances, the absurd logic, the incoherent babble, behind you; that you don't know jack, you are unable most of the time, to distinguish the river from the sea, the sea from the horizon, the horizon from the sky, admit! Embolden, energized by drugs (or perhaps more likely by the lack thereof), lost in the forever-middle of nowhere, on the way to the city-less limits, and ever-changing borderline of waste and debris, what you hear now is the runaway locomotive of your eroding mind: noise, just noise, itself nonsense told to nonsense itself; and noise, before an audience of no-ones and aren't-listening nobodies, sound (and fury), the telling of a tale (an idiot's tale) which, if you really want to know, amounts to not much more, to not much more than, diddly.

Silvia ran with a fast crowd. She appeared on television. Her photograph (usually in the company of her escorts and friends) was always in the newspapers and magazines. Her exploits were hot topic. She and I more than once stayed at the same resort. That's how we met. That's how Silvia and I met. Yes, she was standing, I remember, the first time I laid eyes on her, before a mural depicting a body of water, the surface of which reflected a rain-filled sky. Leaves were dancing on the air. A huge fan blew droplets of moisture onto her hair. They were doing a shoot for a magazine layout. Her portraits adorned the walls. As you entered the lobby, you were greeted by her life-sized (smiling in profile) cardboard cut-out. Whether I spoke to her on that occasion, I'm not sure. No—I did! I did speak to her! It is whether that was the first, or the second time we met, I'm not sure of now. We hit it off right away. Maybe it was the second time. Maybe it was someone who looked like her (hers was the image of the year, that summer everyone looked like her), someone I mistakenly thought was her, it must have been—the first time, the time when it wasn't raining, and she gave me the cold shoulder. Maybe it was fate. Maybe all of this is fate.

Even before we hooked-up, people kept coming up to me saying that I bore a resemblance to her (on-screen, then) constant companion. On one or two occasions, they even mistook me for him, and wanted my autograph. All this attention eventually became too much, too much for me to ignore, too much for me to not seize the ball and run with it. Claiming at times that I was he, and at others, his identical twin, became an obsession. I altered my appearance to further the illusion. Things got out of hand. From newspapers and magazines, I took note of every mention of Silvia and her family. Finding my own name non-intriguing, I told people I would prefer (since I was a soon-to-be-published poet) that they refer to me by my *nom de plume;* it more reflected my inner spirit, I said. Why I chose Rotschild Jarvis—sometimes, Rotchild Hamleton Jarvis—I don't know, except that it was the name I several times inscribed on the bottom of each of the few pages of scrawl in a journal I began writing some years ago (the unfinished manuscript, among my personal items in the locker at the shelter still). I even once, on the strength of my being a 'celebrity', managed to test-drive an expensive automobile. With the ways of the rich, I familiarized myself. I made-up stories. People loaned me money. Maybe they were being kind. Maybe they didn't believe me. Maybe some of them did. Maybe some of them didn't, I don't know. It doesn't matter. Nothing matters. Nothing matters anymore. As it is, I'm under strict medical advice to touch not a drop of alcohol. Yet earlier yesterday (last night, I mean) I had a few. Cognac, it might have been—it *was* cognac! How many I knocked over? I don't know, maybe too many! I didn't handle it well. I didn't handle it at all well! I might have gotten into a fight with someone. At one point, the doggas rode-up on me—they had gotten, they said, a report of someone yelling obscenities and spitting at passing cars. I know how to deal with the doggas. I don't know how to deal with the doggas. Nobody does. I might have passed-out. I did pass-out! An hour or so ago, like Lazarus from the dead I rose, to find myself confused and incoherent of thought, in the muck close to a row of trash-cans between two buildings. My shoulder hurts. Behind my ear, I have a small lump that's painful to touch. How it got there, I don't know. I don't feel well. I smell of garbage. There is blood coming from my body somewhere. One leg of my trousers is soaked. I might have pissed on myself. Maybe I walked in the rain. At my feet, the pools of liquid seem of a reddish hue, as if someone laboring by had bled in them. I might be walking around in a circle. My memory comes and goes. Lately my memory comes and it goes. In the course of a single afternoon, in the middle of conversation with someone, sometimes even in the middle of a sentence, I lose track of what I'm saying. I am being plagued lately too, by a dream, a recurring dream, always the same: Silvia is in the water. Something is wrong. She's an excellent swimmer, yet she seems to be screaming for help, screaming for someone to help her. There are people, there are other boats close-by, but paralyzed with fear, I fail to summon them. I only could watch. A light rain is falling. I am blinded by the rain. Before she goes under, before Silvia goes under for the third time, always just before the third time, I wake-up. I wake-up, and—I'm dreaming still! I'm in a darkened room seated on a chair, with my hands secured behind my back. Someone places a black hood over my head. I am able still to discern, sitting on its haunches, a canine or some such beast, with the camouflaged military boots of a human figure standing by its side. Except for what sounds like the whirring of a great wheel, coming from one corner of the room (or perhaps from one of the adjoining rooms), all is silent. Someone clears his throats. The dog flicks its ears. The light is dimmed. The dog flicks its ears again. The room is plunged in darkness. *IT WAS AN ACCIDENT! AN ACCODENT! THAT'S ALL IT WAS!* It was an accident, I tell you! By claiming that it was otherwise, what gain could there be for anyone! Why won't you believe me! I know that the consensus of opinion is that Silvia is no longer among us. But there is no evidence to support this. One stain does not a murder make! A body was never recovered. No death-certificate exists. Your 'irrefutable facts' prove nothing! In a story like this one, facts seldom indicate the truth; facts by themselves speak not, but like victims silent dead remain; that a tale, that any tale, might be woven around them! Any tale! Silvia is not dead. Silvia is dead no more than these leaves green still of summer, the weather warm we again enjoy, or the stars that nightly gleam. What damage! With a few droplets of blood, what damage you make! Because of your accursed science, what torment I endure!

Of course, Silvia need only appear, she need only enter this room, or walk down the street, and all the hypotheses as to her demise, are out the window, there is no denying that. Facts I do not have—I guess there's no denying that either! But while mine may not be the best of recalls, things hardly a moment passed are from my memory sometimes permanently erased, certain incidents (forgotten by others) are glowing brightly still upon the canvas of my mind: the swollen river, a dim-lit street, the nighttime crowd; the anxious faces that neither this way, nor that way turn; nor left nor right, nor elsewhere glance, but straining, a multitude tirelessly now, dead ahead still to see; each pair of eyes, its own sanctuary, amid the rocks of circumstance, its own crevice, its own refuge, its own shelter from the storm, to secure! These images I have not forgotten. These images I will not forget. Silvia is not yet dead. It was of a night's such chaos, a night as this, that I discovered her; it was on a night such as this (maybe it was this night, maybe this is the same night), that we were separated! Who knows! Now I must find her again. And, if for no other reason but to prove that she existed;

that she existed once; if even only to demonstrate to the local authorities and to the organizers at the shelter, who viewed me both (I suspect) not favorably, I will continue. They were wrong. They were wrong about me! I played no part in Silvia's disappearance. I withhold not now her whereabouts. I am committed only to following leads as I discover them, to reenacting scenarios, overturning stones. I am committed to a re-piling of things, to a re-arranging, to a reassessing of circumstance, with the hopes that one day I would discover what happened; what happened to my memory! Why was I transported secretly — and why so quickly — from one continent to another! Who ordered my surveillance! Having said this, I'll begin. I'll begin again. I'll review the night. And even if none but the blackening of a few pages in my journal should come of it, I'll continue, I'll continue still. I'll note the drop in temperature. I'll survey the frozen river. I'll sift through the debris washed-up along the shore. The poor girl could be at the bottom of the sea. She never was happy in these coastal towns. Their narrow streets and passageways, their hills that seem sloped towards dangerous steep precipices, made her uncomfortable always.

Now like the chirr of insects, now like castanets on the wind, now an ensemble of leaves, green and brown and yellow and gold, sail outwards from the mist; others appear, and quickly, others more, in a painting come-to-life; against a backdrop of river and trees and skyline and sky; their airborne excursion lasting hardly long, like starlings upon a canvas they are spiraled to the ground, vulnerable and silent and motionless and bland, in the path of an on-coming (from both directions) contingent of pounding feet, the naturists, morning joggers and strollers that take advantage of this time of day for their fitness regimen, the damp patterned under-soles of their foot-gear imprinting swiftly already the dried asphalt of the walkway.

It was dark. Night was long. I had been delirious. I imagined a sunrise, discovered myself attending the dawn; tackling the grind ahead, the slime ahead, of another day; moving from bench to bench, trash-can to trash-can, searching for nothing in particular, infuriated when I find nothing in particular; making noises, laughing to myself, laughing out loud; meeting old friends, literally bumping-in to old friends; asking of their families, asking of themselves! How well they looked! How mild the weather! How nice it is that we meet again! Some of them, pretending to not remember me, made themselves deliberately grotesque, and almost into gargoyles turned, before they hurried away; others cringing as they stared, silent remained. I talk to them still. Even when they are unresponsive, even when they attempt to nullify my presence, I talk to them still. How nice! So sorry! Sorry to hear that! So sorry to hear a death in the family—the last thing anyone needs this time of year! Let's stay in touch! Look after yourselves! Look after yourselves, eh! Hey, Bob! Bob! Don't be a stranger, man! Give us a call sometimes! Give us a call!

She mustn't see me! I mustn't let her see me! I'll let her pass. It'll be more fun to let her pass—then, surprise her! I'll surprise her! It'll be more fun! I'll take her in my arms! Silvia! I can't believe it! *Silvia!* I was right! I was right all along! I'll take her in my arms! That's what I'll do! I'll surprise her! She'd' be happy! She'd be so happy to see me. This kind of playfulness, we use to always enjoy! It's been a while! We'll take a photograph. One of the others will have a camera! They'll join-in! Seeing me with Silvia, seeing me and Silvia together again, they'll remember, they'll remember who I am! They'll remember summer! They'll remember the great time we had! They'll join-in—of course, they'll join-in! Of course they will! We had a great time! We'll huddle together. We'll huddle together all of us, all of us close, like we did before! I'll raise my hand in a V for victory sign. V for victory! I'll raise my hand! *Ha! Ha! Ha! Ha! Ha!* I don't beleive it! We'll be happy again. *Ha! Ha! Ha! Ha! Ha!* We were happy! We were all happy. It was summer. We had a great time! What a time we had! The leaves began to fall. My shoulder hurts. There's a ringing in my ear. Then the leaves began to spiral. Bells are ringing in my ear. I must have fallen asleep. I must have been thinking, I must have been thinking only. Sometimes I forget. Sometimes I forget what I'm thinking. I must have been thinking of Silvia. I started in her direction, yet found myself, after innumerable steps, distanced from her only where I'd been still when first I realized that she had arrived on the walkway. She turned pale, and from behind the dark patches that were her her eyes, seemed out-of-focus and underwater still, her flailing arms canceling my advance, forbidding of me, even as I looked towards her, even as I only looked. The others, continuing their strides, appeared (no matter in which direction they were headed) to be receding outwards from my field-of-vision, obliterating not only the space which separated me from them, but with hurried steps and altered demeanor, ensuring that I no longer would recall their names, or that I knew them once; obscuring, eradicating even my last vestiges of memory! I tried to speak, but no voice came. I wanted to move but, without hope or bearing, found myself again, only where I stood.

It is night. People at first, familiar and close, now seemed from their surroundings, even from each other, distant as stars. In every direction they scurried, smiling occasionally nervously, apologetically as if fearing — as if wanting to avoid — contact with each other. Every so often one or two of them would for a few moments stop to inspect the sky (hoping and praying no doubt that the tumult would not come). That it comes, that it comes not, what difference will that make! I authored this script! The rain would come! It would not come! I dreamed this night! I dreamed that it was night! I dreamed that it was not night! I assembled the stars that twinkle in the sky! I obscured them with clouds. I darkened the city streets. I created the shadows. There was no night. There was no crime. There was no crime in the night. None but my own doing all of this is! None but my own doing! Even the portraits of Silvia were created out of my imagination. I invented the crime. I whipped-up the storm. I placed the droplets of blood at the scene, and that they would be washed away, imagined the downpour. I am the sunrise! I am the sea! I am the storm. I am the rotating sky. It is not raining! Look! It no longer is night! The sun no longer shines! The sun never shines! The sun never shines, I say! There's no one on the street! There are no boats on the water, no barges on the river being towed. The Hudson lonely flows! Shadows race along the pier. The tower at Pisa leans. With waves breaking on the rocks, plumes of spray, beads of moisture shooting noiselessly into the sky, the tower at Pisa leans; the sound now of a viola or some such instrument, a flautist, a plucking of strings, feet tapping upon the marble floor, a radio-host clearing his throat, the church on Bloomfield Street being shielded by trees, movement in the narthex, there's movement, a voice coming from the narthex! I know that voice! I know that voice! That's Silvia's voice! That's Silvia! That's Silvia's voice, I tell you! Silvia is in the narthex! She beckons me! Although we've never met, she beckons me still! What am I saying! We *did* meet! We did meet! I tell you we did meet, an eternity ago it seems already—an eternity, though in summer, the throes of summer it only was, as summer is now again, summer still, a summer not yet past, a snapshot being taken, maybe it was; maybe it was yesterday, maybe yesterday was summer, all of summer, all of night, all of warmth and leaves, soft spoken words, edited whispers, by-chance syllables, by themselves coming together, *Silvia!*

Entry: Within a slice of evening, always quick they come! O Cancel them! Banish their glinting countenances, silence their screams, their brays and yelps and shrieks and cries. But, no! Exhausted eyes adjusted not yet to light's sudden departure, see still only the shoddy mess the mind fashions them to see, a carnival of leaves and men, in the cycle of their rituals (faint and silhouetted, as if from within a dungeon or sunken vessel, whose pale-light source, the vagueness of a nightmare or half-remembered long day only permits.) The season they foretell will not come! Perhaps it is already gone. And having caused damage no more than the obscuring of the stars, the threat of a storm, and the rattling of the panes in the window of a room that is sanctuary, the dressed in dour fabrics dwarflike malformed creatures, with icicles and the carcasses of animals for adornment, will their feverish dance suspend; and, descending once more into the abyss from whence they came, leave only the dark, the dark of night, and the night itself.

Goodnight!

Moments ago, a hand reached in from the adjoining room, and turned a switch. A figure in the doorway remains.

Goodnight! Goodnight . . .

Now elusive and non-definable; not wake, not sleep, but undeniable of dreams, on uncomfortable mattresses, ill-fitting cartridges of circumstance lodged in uncompromising here-and-now slots of time.

Goodnight, Gentlemen! Goodnight!

The room is warm. By the stars that shine beyond the

clouds obscuring them, the room is warm; by the allotted increments of a well-run establishment, the corroded
aspirations of God knows how many lives asleep, and
half-asleep, under how many blankets upon the floor; how
many victories, how many adventurous journeys, how
many dark voyages!

Goodnight!

Italy was warm. It was summer. I slept well. I always
sleep well in summer. It isn't summer now; not any more,
it isn't. I'm not in Viareggio. There are no pebbles on the
beach. There are no boats at sea. I'm not walking along
the shore. There are no clouds in the sky; no lightning, no
thunder. It is night. Stars are visible. In the distant north,
stars are gleaming still. There are no crowds in the piazzas. On giant screens no Tosca sings. It isn't raining. There
are no groups of tourists huddled for shelter beneath the
striped awnings; no fountains, no amber lights, no colored
lanterns hanging from the trees. A moment ago, a familiar
voice, *E Lucevan Le Stelle,* in my headset sang. Now there
are no notes in the upper registers; no static, no sound. No
overture, no orchestra! Waves aren't breaking against the
shore, waves aren't breaking, but the cry of a seagull in the
arc of its flight over the bay, over the bay in *Napoli.* It is
summer. It is summer in Naples again; in Genoa again, in
Florence again, in Rome again—it is summer again. Ex-
iting *the Galleria Vittorio Emanuelle* in Milan, I see the
tourists milling in the *Piazza Della Scala.* On the *Via Giuseppe Verde,* a young couple recognize me. They can't
believe their eyes! *Congratulazioni! Congratulazioni,* ex-
citedly they jump and shout. I respond with a V for victory
sign. V for victory! Some of the festivities are already on
the way. *Finally To Be Married,* reads a huge banner hanging from the facade of a near-by building! People are jostling each other for view of the fireworks that would light

the sky. A ship's whistle blows. A ship's whistle blows in the night. The vibrations rattle a set of fluted glasses near a bottle of sparkling wine; cake, a silver tray, presents on a table, a past-her-bedtime young bridesmaid sitting on a chair. The orchestra is in the overture. My shoulder hurts. There's a ringing in my ear. Outside on the damp sidewalk, the footsteps of a passerby is interrupted. There is a ringing in my ear. With the sun not yet risen, a barge is, in the predawn half-light, being hauled away from the pier. On deck, a man is at the rails, his head tilted towards the water. From below the surface, a woman's upper torso, her skin blackened, her hair limp upon her cheeks, her mouth misshapen and agape as in a irrepressible cry, suddenly rises. The man, taken by surprise, almost falls over backwards, and begins now as he regains his footing, to adjust his focus, massaging his eyes with the heels of his palms. The torso is heaved and tossed, but despite the river's flow, the tow of traffic, the under-currents and tide, quickly resubmerges; shifting faintly visibly, in and out of focus, before becoming, totally obscured, as by the depths, it is swallowed again; the water reflecting only now, a starless morning. With the barge swiftly moving, retreated to the housing near the stern, the man watches, pale and askew, a cavalcade of images: the advancing strides of a receding pedestrian, stark trees, gathered clouds, an inverted wavering sky.

Outside on the street, the sound of footsteps begin again, but is overwhelmed this time quickly by a passing vehicle. Damp leaves lash against the panes. The effervescing oceans of sleep and dreams are silent wave upon silent wave encroaching. A chorus of sighs and moans and grunts and rasps, fills the room. The windows timorous millimeters shift and clink. With the weight of one of the staff ascending to the upper floor, the wooden stairwell creaks. Someone farts out loud. My headset works. The overture ends. The curtain is about to rise. Now that the curtain is about to rise, my headset is working again. The opera begins. Scarpia's fleeing figure is by lightning illuminated! My shoulder hurts. The audience is hushed. The flautist trills. In the *Piazza Della Scala,* the figures that moments ago scurried are in their strides halted now, and turned to monuments of stone. All is silent. A carjacker is killed. Shah lives in Brooklyn. A cellphone falls onto the floor. Europe is saddened. Summer ends. Afloat on a fire of shredded documents, I hear the sound of castanets, laughter, a woman's voice, her infectious cry. It nearly is night. In a snapshot framed, Silvia and I and the others are on a beach together close. Our arms entwine. We are smiling. As the wind picks-up, a miscellany of leaves, scraps of paper, candy-wrappers and tiny pieces of debris becomes airborne. Someone says something that our voices in laughter swell. Our gazes turn towards the sky. I'm dreaming. The clouds are hanging low; that they would darken and turn to rain, I'm dreaming. I'm dreaming again, I'm dreaming still. And though I might wake to find that it isn't raining, or that it hasn't rained; to watch the sky as it clears, to watch the clouds rolling away, I still would wake. I would wake, and fix my focus; I would fix my focus on the sky. Yes I would fix my focus on the sky. And if the sky was not of summer, I would remember summer. I would remember summer still. I would remember Silvia, and I would remember summer. For Silvia was summer, as summer was Silvia; as summer is summer still, a clinging patina, not yet discarded mementos; redolence and rust, the ghost of an affair off-track gone, summer, summer still. I would adjust my stance. Yes, I would adjust my stance, and I would fix my focus; and making sure that my feet are firmly planted on the ground, I would shrug my shoulders. At Silvia and at summer, I would shrug my shoulders. Even at Silvia, even at summer, even at the sky, even at the stars; even at the stars that shine, I would shrug my shoulders; yes, even at the stars that shine! For the stars always shine. When they are obscured by clouds, they shine. Whether we gaze towards them or not they shine. Even when day's light blinds us, and we are by our own selves eclipsed, they shine. They are shinning now. They are shinning still. Tosca is singing. They are shining still. Even as Tosca sings, they are shinning still! As Scarpia will die! They are shining still. Even as Silvia will die! Even as one day even I will die! Even as the stars are shinning! Even as they are shinning brightly! Even as the stars are shining brightly still . . .

Ned Ned & Other Poems

NED NED

Of loved-ones lost
To ourselves we sometimes say
I wish he were still alive
I wish she was still alive

All the dead of all of time
If they could speak
they too would say
We wish we were still alive
We wish we were still alive

A slave among wandering barbarians
Than king of all the dead
I'd rather be said
Agamemnon

We're born to die
At birth our eulogies we cry
And walk as long as we may live
Ever close beside the grave

SORCERY OF THE DAY

Battered objects salvaged from the fray
A sentry standing night by day
The crafty hound that makes no sound
Save in a garbled treacherous way

On time-worn ever-traveled lines
Tenacious heroes bide their time
Hawkers in a frenzied way
Imprinting images in the clay

Smoke thundering with the din of war
Derelicts squandered on a far-off shore
In anger rise and cry again each day
Damn the hunter and the prey!

Before a self-proclaimed empire
Amesmered alignavecs aspire
To image-mongers ransom pay
Sorcery this is
     the sorcery of the day!

RHYTHM-A-NING

We Speak not of heroes
With Troy the age of heroes ended
And as Zeus had promised
                              a new age
The iron-age of men began

We Speak of men
Of their poems and of their songs
And of the things they shape
And of the things they shaped to come

Jordu Mildama Brownie's Spring
Moody's Mood Trane's Reign Sonny's Airegin
Lester's Leap Miles's Modes Denzil's Move
Birks Wirks Klook's Klique Bags Groove

Monk's Bemsha Juan Tizol's Conga Brava
Chano Pozo's Manteca Boptura Bloomdido Aleutia
Oscar Pettiford's Oscalypso Ornette's The Sphinx
George Russel's Ezz-thetics Budo an Ice-cream
Konitz

Elmo's De-dah Tad Dameron's Dameronia
Mingus' Ah Um Eric So Long Junkas Juks Juba
Horace's Ecaroh Bean's Picasso A taste of funji
Bobo's Beat Blue Mongo Afro Ogunde

Of men yes of men We Speak
Of their mettle and of their mold
Their Points of Departure
And of the venues they would hold

Café Bohemia A Night in Tunisia
Cecil at the Montmatre Sun Ra's Overtones of China
Hair on end on the heads of those within earshot
Of Roy Haynes in a darkened room
                        that was the Five Spot

And if too often with reverence still
It is only because among things we hail
There are some we cherish more
More than heroes more than men
                      more than iron-men

AIN'T THAT JOE

Ain't that Joe
  ain't that Joe!
On a morning in the city
When he walked and talked
Ain't that Joe!

The grainy images
That was evening's flow
Careless laughter in a picture-show
Ain't that Joe!

Wait up Joe
  wait-up!
At least I'm sorry let me say
Without the wind I've been for all my days
An empty staff upon which a banner none
did raise

Ain't that sea
Ain't that sky
Aren't those sea-gulls
With the clouds beyond them scudding by

The rotted ribs on an old ship bogged
A helmsman at the helm
An entry in the log
Ain't that Joe!

TUM VITA

Tum vita
Cut unkindly as you will
In solace night
Day's heft pains me still

Aur tum bai
Stay not silent dead
Wake
walk again
Hear the songs we did in yon-times sing

Cold krail supper
I know now unruly stones
The tedious dirt
Of an empty trail

Respite tum vita
     respite
That I might if even only in a dream
The face once more of my brother see
Instead of always in the mirror
                    only me

THE LOG (ARMED-FORCES)

The bitter akara
A steep hill climb
Gruesome casualties
We daily find

Corpses underfoot
Like rotted leaves
Among them still
The faces once of colleagues

On tours of duty
Where we must go
Not many will tread
Few dare follow

We relish this task
Take us often it will
Not just into shit
But deep in kaka still

MOP MOP

Hizzip-trizzip/hizzip-trizzip
Hizzip-trizzip/hizzip-trizzip (mop-mop)
Trak-trizak/trak trizak
Trak-trizak trak/trak trizak

Trak-trak/trak-trak/trak-trak/trak-trak
Trak-trak/trak-trak/trak trizak-trak
Trizak-trizak/trizak-trizak
Trizak-trizak/trizak-trizak

Ching-ching/ching-ching/ching-ching/ching-
ching
D-cymbal ring/ching-ching ching-ching
D-cymbal ring/d-cymbal ring
D-cymbal ring/ching-ching ching-ching

Jizam jam/mboom mboom
Jizam jam/mboom boom boom
Mboom boom boom/mboom boom boom

Jizam-jam/mboom boom boom
Klizip-klizip/klizip-klizip/klizip-klizip
Klizip-klizip/klizip-klizip/klizip-klizip
Krrr-krrr/krrr-krrr/Krrr-krrr/krrr-krrr
Duddup dup/duddup dup/updup dup dup
updup dup dup

IN THE NIGHT
(TWO WOMEN SPEAK)

Let the world see what I see
Let them hear what I hear
Let them see it again
Let them hear it again
                    let them deny it again

Of their indifference forgive them
Emmit Till and Albert Ayler's years
Are vintages by-gone let them say
Ours is a better flavor
                    we live a brighter day

Up high in the poplar tree
Dark blood on the leaves still see
Hanging spoiled a rotting fruit
The tangled mess upon the root

And of a body floating on the river
The figure turning with the wind
Fire on the hill
                the sickening vile odor
Ask them still!

THE GIRL IN THE BEEMER RED RIDE

How smoothly the car runs
Into the lot it turns
The beemer red ride
A pretty girl drives

With tires black and silver trim
Comes to rest beside a wall within
She'll exit now and pretty smile
While on her cell she chats and styles

Men with age silly and frail
Near beautiful women are sillier often still
They seldom get their wish and never learn
Even if they do
            they'll into idiots turn

How smoothly the car runs
Upon the ramp it climbs
The beemer red ride a pretty girl drives
Her companion kool and quiet at her side

410 CHELSEA

Winter you
Warmth was you
Your kisses in the spring
Were joyous too

The wine of autumn
Danced with you
Leaves cascading
Even as the summers flew

The color of a ribbon
Through my fingers slipping
 A lingering ghost
 A nightly showing

 In the falling rain
 An umbrella true
 Were thoughts of you
 And the quiet shelter
                    of your smile

OUTWARD BOUND

Even as you lift-off!
Of unremembered excrescence
A comet's tail dogs you still
Look homeward Earthon
Than regions in Kosmos far
Regard a planet you'll distance more
Rather than a continent new
Of contingents old discover
Yourselves of legions lost
From your cockpit high
A mirror glance Earthon
It is you who are alien now!

MEMO

We came
We saw
He died
Even of a fellow-creature
Complacent still the woman Hillary did say
Earthons are nurturers of kill-power
A star upon their banner
A feather in their cap
Of frontiers in pursuit
Forever steps they'll take
You are mortal
And in Kosmos elsewhere exist
Careful watch
Unto your world
When they would come
How quickly you will see
How quickly you will die!

A KILL IN HARLEM

Mumu was right there when it happened
The poor child saw Gerry being killed
Word on the street was that Ricky did it
And no one would go against Ricky

A new-jack gang wanted in
At first they reasoned with Gerry
Let us off a bundle or two they say
Give us the slowest hours of the day

Gerry didn't see it that way
                              he laughed in their faces
Those kids wasn't going to accept that
They got some money together
                              and they paid Ricky
The rest now everyone knows is history

Some say Gerry didn't have to die
Others that his dope was good
Mumu who couldn't speak
Watched from where she stood

DEBBIE YOU MEAN?

Yes when Debbie is happy she is pretty
She seems always pretty
Is she always happy?
No one is always happy

Anyway whether happy she is
Unhappy she is
Debbie she is
Pretty still she might be

To be unhappy and pretty
Is usually not easy
Of features pleasant some women remain
Even when they are sad or angry

When Debbie is ecstatically happy
Is she extremely pretty?
Data of such nature would be
To me I'm sorry to say
                    not privy

A MAN UNHEARD FROM LONG

Is there victory sweeter
Than that of a man unheard from long
His enemies thinking they had done him in
Believed he would be forever gone

With close friends fearing him dead
How in peculiar ways
Things sometimes happen
He surfaces to say instead

Forgive that I am deceased not yet
I promise in the future
One day I surely will be
As would we all I guess

Of old wine now let's drink
And as we set fire to the past
A game of dominoes friendly enjoy
Atop the marble of my tomb

YOU JAQUELINE

Was it you in the evening
Was it the evening in you
The shapes and sounds you sculptured
Even heaven nurtured

Was it in a fragrance
Was it in a flower
Was it only fragrance
The fragrance of a flower

The color of silence
The symbol and the form
Resounding nuances
Rhythm that seem hardly wrong

It was evening and it was you
It was you in the evening
It was the evening in you
It was you
            in the you of you—Jacqueline

ANDROMEDA

A sea of stars
A milky way
Sky and night
The ocean's sway

A shining light
A crested hill
A grid of streets
Coastal village still

Nuanced syllables of a name
       Perseus will hear
Perseus will hear
Daughter of Cepheus
Perseus will hear

Was dark Andromeda
Andromeda that was
Andromeda Dark
Andromeda
    Andromeda

ONE FOR DERRICK (?)

Had it out-done the train
The horse that failed could victory claim
Forgetting not of course
That the train is but an iron horse

That non-competitive with others ride
On rails together side by side
At journey's end to observe as one
The trackless indifference of a world beyond

No scroll no parchment kind
No future formula we would find
Or digital board on which to draw
A travel mode efficient more

But a horse with wings up in the sky
A rider in the saddle galloping by
Below him relict on the shelves
The dreams we dreamed beyond ourselves

DREAD TODD DADA

Na light in darkness pin-point shine
Na wisp o' sound das quiet puncture
Invisible mum a presence
Ever at me door

In breakfast bread
Constant a table place
Sho na frown
Nar scowl nar grimace face

Monster vile
Ousland shroud that harry
Back now kom
Time's gate rile and tarry

Nar just you but solemn say
Others too and others mo
Meself I'll sho
In den kommenden jahren

OF FIVE GUYS NAMED CARL SOVERAL

That we were up against a dirty fighter
Who never quits and doesn't tire
Or even that his name was life
We paid no attention to the rumor

Like the lyrics in a song
We breezed along
And when challenged surmounted still
The awkward-most daunting hill

The rumors turned out to be well-founded
We standing eight-counts took
The rhythm floundered
Someone the bell of laughter stole

Where did our buoyancy go
What key is this
The changes in tempo
To anticipate them how could we have failed

Damn you suddenly now we're saying
Damn you life that kicks us when we're down
Damn you death that takes us all
Damn you life!

TO NONE ALIGNED

Worshipers of noise and fire
We heeded your imperatives
Did we not make way for your serried ranks
Who can dispute your right

But for a canon's bright glow
Not even the torrent you see
Nor all the corpses borne
Nor a veil of tears that is ours

We ask not the tally
Who their parents were
How they worship
           from whence they came
Grief we only know is human

And that a companion betrays you
Custodian of kill-power
Betrays you every day
Rampant death running still
               its wanton ways

PANSTRUM DENSTRUM

Upon the metal of a drum
A tuner stays his hammer hand
Hearing intently now instead
Zidjian romps inside his head

With virtuosi camped beside his door
He dents the notes and listens more
Delighting all who came to see
Playing briefly now a rhapsody

One phrase dances in its flight
Leaping adventurous like the stars of night
Up and down a dextrous run
Ending now with a riff and strum

The sounds random even
With their instruments men create
Sweeter than a kiss
Will music sometimes make

THE WAITING DARK
(NEW YORK, 2010)

Speak! Speak O Locks
You whispered then
Life's hand heavy oppresses me
Lost I am amid a galaxy of stars

The weight of all solitude I would bear
Into the labyrinth venture
That I would hear again your voice
Upon this lonely river

Beyond the silence of its forbidden surface
Sound only from your lips carry
The mist and clouds
                    its distant banks
Are ever yours

Is it out of Tartarus you came
Speak!
Speak O locks!
Speak now
Speak again

THE FAR

We waited someone
Who when he came was dread
With locks so full
They obscured the sky

That the sun turned cold
And for a period how long
No one could tell
All light refused to shine

The earth stood still
And covered with ice
The rafts-man prospered
Dead souls reigned

By tremors we were rocked
When they subsided
The lights had returned
And the sky filled again with stars

HERESTADT (2016)

Tram tram tram
SitRam SitRam
Jagnaat Wajank
Tram tram stride
Das tinsel drum
Jute das blackguard speil
Rawan ka nam
Human das splatam
Nar common genocide —
Das splatam splat
Das splatam splatam
Das splatam splatam splatam!

OF INFANTUMAN

Even
In the mirror of his madness
No one spoke
Distanced from the stars
Alone in the dark
Within himself imprisoned
Amid groans and gripes
And burps and farts
And sneezes and coughs and cries
The feces he excreted
And from the debris of a dream
Of demons and gods
And heroes and men
A tale he nansed
A curious tale
But no one spoke
No one
No one

A Station in Midgard

With light from its underbelly painting the surrounding walls, ceiling and fixtures, a near-blinding silver, the train entering the station seemed, for brief moments, a reptilian behemoth racing noisily along the tracks. Approaching its customary stop besides the platform, the aluminum-and-glass ribbon-like raucous blur is slowed; and, as the intermittent bright flashes subside, a succession of creaks, clanks, screeches and prolonged hisses, replace the near-colossal thunder with which moments ago it exited the tunnel. In the interior of the cars, shadows assume shape, depth and color; hats, coats, shoulders and sleeves, backpacks and carry-on items come into focus; discernible now too, are the faces of passengers; some already on their feet waiting for the sliding doors to open; some, with their heads in newspapers, magazines and electronic-devices, remain seated. Others, seemingly indifferent to their surroundings, are almost frozen beside them; and—even as the grinding symphony of screeches and squeaks (to which the loud rails had given way) abruptly ends; even as the doors several times repeatedly loudly open and close—continue still to stare vacantly ahead, unaware perhaps of their being halted unusually long, or even that they are motionless still, inside the dim fog of an afternoon in a tunnel under the ground.

Nothing much happens here. One of the few still-functioning stops along the once-celebrated National Line of almost a century ago, the Station at Midgard, has been slated (since God knows when) for closure. And how much longer it will exist in its unpredictable lim-bo of unsatisfactory service is anyone's guess. But for a during the work-week, twice-a-day truncated rush-hour, the cars are never at capacity. And today (a slightly more crowded Thursday than usual), is no exception. It is mid-afternoon. The boarding passengers are seated. While a handful of disembarking ones, already on the platform, are heading hastily towards an illuminated red exit-sign, above the arched-entrance to a narrow passageway, with-in which (separated by varying degrees of shadow and poor-visibility), a row of ceiling-fixtures dispense about four or five equidistant cones of faint light onto the floor. The disparate group of nervous-looking travelers cut, one after the other, in and out of these pale shafts, like scurry-ing extras in a science-fiction action-movie; and, as they begin ascending a set of metal stairs that sharply wind, are swallowed head-first by the cloud of darkness hanging there from above.

The doors close. A minute goes by—maybe two, maybe more. They open again; they close again. Ten min-utes. Nothing. Fifteen. The train is stalled. In one of the middle cars, the conductor is, as much as his cramped compartment will allow him, shuffling around, commu-nicating perhaps with the Center For Control (CFC), or with the operator at the head of the train, while depressing one of the buttons on the panel in front of him, again and again. Finally he stops, steps out of the compartment, and, locking the doors behind him, begins walking hurriedly through the cars.

Disrupting one of these trains shouldn't be difficult. A solid small object, strategically-placed, carefully con-cealed near the rails, application of a number of easy-to-get-hold-of electronically-controlled devices, could cause a problem. Until the problem is solved (in this case, until the conductor could safely close the doors), the train will not move. Other trains are soon affected. Before you know it, a limited area, both below and above ground, would be compromised, the density of individuals within its perimeters, increased several fold; not a comforting prospect these days. Anyone bent on destruction, and ruthless enough to take advantage of this kind of know-how could, if circumstances allow him, cause large-scale chaos; not to mention blood-spill, perhaps even death, heartache, and grief. Of all this, the station-man, a short, recessive, aging (but at the same time fairly robust-looking) figure, not visible until now; standing (or more likely moving imperceptibly slowly) on the platform near the tail-end of the train, is acutely aware. In his tenure with the National Rail & Road Corporation (most of the time at Midgard, or one of its sub-stations) he absorbed what must easily amount to a sizable dossier of important data regarding not only the many 'accidents' that could interrupt the fluidity of the trains, but as to the thousand and one things that can—and, on a daily basis do, in fact—go wrong within the vast network of the aged and deteriorating transportation system itself. (Over the years he witnessed a lot of laughable stuff, too.) Still, no one is more aware than he, that despite the bunch of keys he must at all times carry—the hammer in his locker, the senseless oversized gloves, the ridiculous, forever ill-fitting uniform; the silver shield, the numbers on his shirt-front, the epaulets and what not—his position is little more than that of (that he was himself) a glorified trash-collector. He knows, moreover, that should he, at any point, of this crucial fact, become unmindful, or be so bold (there were times, when he would have been) as to espouse, or even defend, ideas that conflicted with those of his higher-ups, the NRRC (or *NERK* as generally they are called) would, in any number of drastic ways, be more than willing to remind him.

Having not yet completed his survey of the cars, the conductor is attempting to placate a passenger who like a jack-out-of-a-box, had sprung from his seat to challenge him; and who, from all appearances, was not in agreement with his line of reasoning. Observing their animated confrontation, the station-man shakes his head and smiles. He gives them his back. Over the years, he's had his share of derisive comments from irate patrons, and wants now to ignore the stalled train with its frantic conductor, and increasingly restless passengers. The scenario hardly ever changes. The passenger gets a few things off his chest. He then calms down. The conductor returns to his compartment. He goes through the rigmarole of using the communications system. He depresses the button on the panel in front of him. He sticks his head out the window, he scans the platform; he adjusts his cap, he loosens his collar. He swears under his breath. He looks out the window again. He scratches his temple. He whistles out loud, as if to say, 'Shit! We have a problem, here!' To the station-man, this is nothing but theater. He's seen it all before.

Everything from sun-tan lotion, to after-dinner snacks, to seltzer water, is advertised on the walls of the station. And it is to this gallery of colorful posters that the station-man, determined not to be bothered by the stricken train, directs his attention. With glistening beads of moisture clinging to her pearl-gray flawless skin, a porcelain young girl is stepping out of the water, against a backdrop of sea and surf and horizon and sky. The diaphanous fabric of her swim-wear (the upper half anyway) being wet, reveals the twin hemispheres of her breasts, their erectile nipples, the darker-colored circular area of flesh surrounding them. Whether the same is true for the lower half, is not apparent, since it is there in the region of the abdomen and upper thigh, that a 'vandal' has struck several times with whatever weapon he wielded, lacerating, almost amputating her right leg; attacking the poster with such ferociousness, that huge chunks of its sub-strata, pieces of the station wall, some with fragments of bright colored paper glued to them, are lying still on the floor. The station-man picks up one of these pieces of 'evidence', and for some inexplicable reason, squeezes it between his thumb and index finger; to discover that he has drawn blood. Whoever did this can't be far. He is either on the train, or perhaps lurking in the exit passageway linking the platform with the street above. The station-man looks around. He sees no one. He looks at the paralyzed train. Someone had attempted to scribble, but had not finished, what probably was meant to be two words: (the first, beginning with a huge S, followed by a lower-case vowel, before becoming blemished; the second, but the broken tail of an exaggerated elongated flourish coming out of an ellipse, on the side of one of the cars). The station-man is uncomfortable with this, and feels an overwhelming apprehensiveness, that even the candle-lit atmosphere in which a formally-dressed young couple is enjoying a box of chocolate wafers; nor the green and purple giant from whose fingertips arcs of light illuminate a row of gabled-houses in a bleak meadow, nor the equally-innocuous succession of posters which follow—fail to alter. He looks again at the blood on his fingers. He decides to move with a little more purpose, but has no idea where he's going, or precisely what he intends to do. He feels faint. For the better part of twenty years, under even the most adverse circumstances, he effortlessly maneuvered the difficult recesses of this station, but collides violently now with a pair of red-painted fire-buckets, as if he hadn't noticed that they were filled with sand, or that they protruded from their fixtures on the wall. He rests his forehead on the back of one hand (the palm flat against a tiled section of wall); with the other he feels for his heart. Breathing slightly irregularly, he mutters something to himself, something which sounded like, 'Oh no! Not again!'

That it was he, those many years ago, who discovered the young girl's body always seemed—seems to this very day—somewhat strange. She came through the station regularly on week-day afternoons, sometimes with a male companion, sometimes with one or two of her girlfriends. When in the passageway he had come upon what at first he thought was a mannequin on the floor, a couple of the easily-accessible low-wattage screw-type light bulbs directly over-head had (as nowadays often happens) been tampered with—had gone out, causing the already poorly-lit passageway to be further darkened. He re-adjusted them, and the lights immediately came back on; but, inexplicably, failed to relay this fact to the authorities when they interviewed him. Even when at one juncture, a detective had the lights several times switched on and off, to demonstrate a point, he remained silent. Robbery was not a motive. The investigation hinged on two theories: a 'crime of opportunity' committed by a deranged stranger; or, a (secret perhaps) romantic liaison gone sour, the work of an (unknown to others) male companion with whom the victim might have had a falling-out, and who could have accompanied, or followed her, into the station on that particular day. To make matters worse, the longer he withheld what little he remembered, the more he realized how severely he could be affected by its belated disclosure. Change your story once in response to official questioning nowadays, and you are forever painted as someone who should not be trusted. The station-man knows this. He knows a lot of things. He prides himself on his ability to adjust to the 'climate' of the times. Like most people he's aware, for instance, of the current rumored existence of foreign saboteurs (perhaps imagined, perhaps real) on 'local soil', as is usually officially in the mass-media amplified. But, unlike most people, he knows that the fragile national nervousness (which borders often on a particularly obtuse form of hysteria) is as fickle as the wind; and that, at its worst, it invariably gift-wraps a freer hand to those in power—a hand which, with a swift mind of its own, falls indiscriminately whimsically whenever and wherever it chooses. A long story short: these were not the best of times, to find oneself at the wrong end of the savage kosh authorities regularly bring to bear upon the heads of those suspected of being complicit in the simplest of crimes, let alone murder. He's had his brushes with the law. He knows that, whereas in the old days, an earnest investigator, allowing the facts to lead where they might, would regard no one (and thus, everyone) as suspect; present-day law-enforcers rely instead on the far more accessible and, naturally, more rewarding route of collaring an 'easy mark', in other words, some-one whose circumstance they perceived (often not without good reason) to be more vulnerably malleable.

Then there was the matter of his employ. Once it had become apparent that the intensity of the investigation had diminished, helped in part by the social status and ethnicity of the dead girl—the daughter of insignificant, not particularly attractive, dark-skinned immigrants with difficult sounding names—he was given a new uniform (a shirt with epaulets) and reassured that while 'station maintenance' was undoubtedly his prime responsibility, he was at all times a 'representative', of the NRRC transportation system and that his 'greater function', was to watch over and protect all who made use of its services. By a man he had never seen before, but who was obviously someone of authority, with a refined (though at times not easy to understand) manner of speaking, who also wore an expensive tie, and was no doubt from 'down-town', he was reminded that 'we' were not yet all the way out of danger; and that should it be demonstrated that 'we' had 'nourished' an atmosphere that 'facilitated' the perpetrating of a crime, 'we' could be facing civil, perhaps even criminal litigation. Finally the man in the suit, after saying something he didn't quite understand, shook his hand, glanced around the station, several times, wrote something down on a piece of paper, and concluded: 'You're doing a fine job. Keep it up!"

A stalled train, electrical failure, flooding on the tracks, a disabled passenger being removed by paramedics from one of the cars; a dimmed, flickering light-bulb about to go, unusual fresh graffiti, the sudden uncovered crustiness of a metal object welded long in the dirt beside an abandoned tool-shed in a little-used section of the rail-yard—any single one of these occurrences; the bleak atmosphere of the station itself, the dust-filled almost always near-deserted caverns, could on any given day, reignite, and often vividly evoke in his mind, the savage brutality of that afternoon (that Thursday afternoon) those many years ago, and the part he played in it. That a young girl had been murdered on his watch was bad enough. He without reason withheld information that might have been relevant, this was even more disturbing. But what troubled him most, when he looked back upon it, was what he saw as the reasons for his unusual behavior: what he saw of himself.

As a young man with a slightly-blemished record (two convictions for being in the possession of controlled substances), he had made the sobering move of finding a decent job. He joined the NRRC. Back then, theirs was a policy (long since discontinued) that required two years of satisfactory service before employment would be considered permanent. Within this period, an employee may be dismissed without explanation. (He had not yet completed his probationary stretch, as this was taking place.) In a number of subtle ways his superiors communicated how they wanted him to respond to official questioning, how they wanted the 'incident' as they called it, to be handled. 'Not without caution' was, during the many briefings, the guiding phrase his superiors impressed upon him most.

Perhaps it was the fear of losing his job; perhaps it was a basic lack of character that forced him to behave in the manner in which he did. Whatever it was, he could never face the dead girl's relatives. They weren't fooled. They knew he wasn't telling all. During a brief encounter with the family, one of the younger boys—the near-image of his murdered sibling—tried to spit on him, and had to be restrained by family members (who themselves seemed ready, together with a few sympathizers, to cause a disturbance near the administrative building in which the inquest was held). In the end, they left quietly. But since that day, wherever he went, their scornful faces churned, as if on a lake of fire, before him; their looks of contempt he knew, no matter what, would never go away. On his shoulders too, the anvil of his non-gallant behavior those many years ago, with each passing day, grew heavier and heavier still. It was as if, he in his darker moments felt, his own hands had groped and violated the young girl's flesh, his fingers had encircled her throat; and, even as she choked and gasped in the darkened passageway, had applied pressure; fastening his grip more tightly, stronger and stronger, harder and harder, until she stopped struggling, and gasped, as the last breath left her, and she rested near-weightless, in his arms. Was he—the question often troubled him whenever he was alone—the one who murdered her, who really murdered her . . .

These delays, though they occur frequently, seldom lasts long. And while the extended presence of the train—with its conductor, operator, and irascible passengers (God knows who among them), its interminable announcements—often made him uncomfortable, the station-man knew that whatever the reason for this particular one, the train would be moving shortly. And at any rate, even if it didn't, there wasn't anything he could do that would expedite its departure. His concern now is with a problem of a more graspable nature—one over which he at least had some measure of control. He could see that one of the lamps inside the exit-passageway had gone out. And, judging by the dimness of the shaft of light projected onto the platform, perhaps a second lamp (one not visible from where he stood) was also malfunctioning. No sooner had he entered the passageway, he discovered that this was precisely the case; and, as he ascended the stairs, realized that a third lamp was at the very moment being threatened: The silhouetted outline of a huge masculine figure was standing directly beneath it, with one arm extended above his head. The huge gloved-hand already partially obscuring the light seemed ready to take hold of the lamp. 'HEY! HEY! HEY!' the station-man shouted, stumbling as he does so. 'What are you doing?' He thought he saw the hand beginning to rotate, but then the lights went out. For the moments that followed, he might as well have been—it fact he was—completely blinded.

The feminine heels descending from above had stopped. Perhaps realizing that there was something not quite right about the stairs and tunnel, the girl hesitated, so that her eyes would adjust to the unusual conditions. But silence . . . silence, then a gasp, a few short, barely-audible sounds, a woman's voice, definitely a woman's voice, was all that followed. Had she, despite her assailant's attempts to contain her response (and undoubtedly that's what happened) managed, as she wrestled with him on the darkened stair, those last cries, only that they too would be muffled quickly, before ceasing altogether, the voice, methodically deadened; all but the most basic of movement, the arms that flail, the chest that heaved, eventually even the blood that flowed within the veins and arteries, constricted. The tiny creature now hardly more than a brittle, scaled-down mannequin, in the grip of two massive arms, one gloved-hand effectively covering the nostrils and mouth, the other sealing the passage within the throat, obstructing the flow of air; the shoulders, fore-arms, upper arms and torso becoming increasingly non-human, coiled into a single destructive device, exerting its savage force. The mannequin, the station-man remembers, had managed, an additional soft short cry. That's when the neck must have snapped.

The conductor re-opened the doors, allowing a nondescript man carrying an overstuffed briefcase (he had dashed out of the exit), onto the train. Safe inside, the late-comer offered a silly grin to no one in particular, then stuck his head and shoulders back outside the still-open doors in what might have been a nod of gratitude (or even a gesture of annoyance), directed at the conductor at the middle of the train. Whatever had been his intent, the doors at the same time began to close, causing him to spill, as he abruptly withdrew, some of the contents of his briefcase (gloves, pen-and-ink notes with huge red asterisks on yellowish legal-sized pages) onto the floor. The station-man meanwhile, unable to determine whether the figure who all but knocked him off his feet had attempted to do so deliberately, and was the same one he saw tampering with the lights before they went out, or a passenger frantically trying to catch the train—is down on one knee still. On hearing the doors close, he decides it was more likely the latter, and begins to pick himself up from the floor. As he's attempting to do so, he notices while reaching for his cap (fallen beside him), something which caused him almost to lose his balance again: out of the darkness on the stairs, a young girl's forearm half-extended into the air. Even in the poor light, he could see the fingers curled, blood beginning at the wrist, already forming a tiny pool in the middle of the upturned palm before trickling through the fingers unto the floor below: the face and shoulders and arms close at his feet, the rest of the body, upper-more, less clearly discernible in the darkness on the stairs. In his confusion he is uncertain whether he should attend first to the lights (one of his solemn duties), or rush to the girl's assistance. He would help the girl. But in the darkness even as he advanced; even as he drew closer to the disheveled matted hair, the expression-less eyes, the colorless cheeks and parted lips, something seemed to be telling him to be cautious; he already was, he realized, too late . . .

At worst, he might have smeared the already stained body with (remembering his bleeding thumb) blood of his own. Absolving himself from what others were certain to perceive as complicity would not be easy, not this time. On both knees now, he runs his hand several times over the logo on his cap (the letters NRRC in raised golden thread struck by a thunderbolt inside an ellipse with wings), as if it were some sort of talisman that would power him out of the frightful circumstance in which he now found himself! The security of the commuters—the man in the suit had reminded him—was in his hands! Within the perimeters of the underground—at least here in Midgard, he ruled. He tried. Over the years, he tried. Even though at times he felt as if all the security of all the world was his—he tried. He made his mistakes. But as sure as Wednesday spawned Thursday, he tried. Now there was nothing he could do. He saw the absurdity of his position—saw ev-erything suddenly so vividly. A ghost-like bedraggled fig-ure now appeared and as if in consolation, knelt in the darkness beside him. He look upon its face; upon the wisps of gray, the recessed cheeks; the indentations at the temples, the veins welling on the forehead; beads of sweat streaming down the neck, and realized that he was look-ing at himself—or his father! He had somehow acquired the ability to see his own image, to see himself, as if from outside himself, to see the present and future at the same time. He appeared almost non-human; and, in the poor light, resembled a wolf baying at the moon. Yet from the misshaped rhombus of his parted lips not even a whis-per came. Nor could he when he placed his hand over his breast or felt his wrist, detect a heart-beat or pulse (the price no doubt for his sudden metamorphosis). His brain ignited, the thought came to him: Snakes must die! That's what the graffiti artist was trying to say! He was himself, it dawned on him too, already deceased; a restless ghost, linked forever to a murder committed ages ago (perhaps one he himself had committed) within the entrails of a decades-closed obscure station, derelict and forgotten in a bleak city, through which now only a slag-laden dilapidated work-train occasionally passes, and sometimes for a brief period rests, before dimly continuing its tortuous ponderous way, to inch again; clanking and creaking and gasping, and grinding; a mammoth wounded exhausted *metalon,* breathing flames, spitting its sparks, enduring as he too now must endure, the torment of a journey undeniable and inexorable, an ingress fiery and clangorous, within the foundries of hell!

He could not hear himself. Try as he might, he could not hear himself. When he cried for help, a sound of a greater intensity each time nullified his voice, and made it inaudible: the departing train, thundering on down inside the tunnel . . .

The Ice-cream Van

When the van arrives, the crescendo of cries that began with the sounding of its chimes, diminishes, *modulate* might be a better word; yes, they quickly modulate into the rascally voices of children at play. They're having a good time. They always have a good time. 'Wadtzup! Ice-cream man,' one of them would say. A burst of laughter would follow. Another voice echoes the first, laughter again and, of course, 'Wadtzup, Ice-cream man! Wadtzup!' again. Comes a frenzy with the younger kids jockeying to be first at the window. All would be quiet again soon. All is quiet now. The van has not yet arrived. Nor are the chimes sounding. The Ice-cream man does not come every day. He could be around the corner; or he could be far away, on another street, perhaps in another part of town, in attend of another bunch of kids; dispensing with his customary dexterousness, the wafered cones and napkins, the flavored syrup, the sprinkled topping, placing the tiny wooden pallets, atop the mounds of chocolate, and vanilla, and strawberry, and marzipan . . .

In addition to its tasty promise, the ice-cream van's arrival often signals an end to much of the morning's activities. The sounding of its chimes represent the start to a second period for the day (one less hectic than the first). By the time the van departs, the children will have abandoned their play (centered now, because of the temperatures, around the open hydrant on the far side of the street); accompanied by their adult guardians, whose watchful eyes are never far, they would, after carefully washing their hands, retreat often for a siesta or snack within the air-conditioned comfort of their homes, or with electric-fans and iced-drinks on the tables before them, sometimes remain chill, in the shaded gardens beside the row of houses on the less stifling side of the street.

August afternoons are often unbearable—unbearable, and irresistible and beautiful. It is a few minutes past one. Glittering coins of dancing light are already vying with the silhouetted foliage of trees on the scorched sidewalk and street, the spewing hydrant painting a jagged, ever-changing liquid line that seems at times to separate asphalt from concrete; its narrow band of dark moist cool flowing nonchalantly downhill. There is a breeze. Near the fan in my window, close to the ensemble sculpture from Benin, the cluster of clay pots with their veritable forest, the cacti and ferns, and miniature palms, I am watching the children play. There is hardly a breeze. In his apartment directly above (identical to my own, though undoubtedly far more cluttered), the old man is watching, too. He knows when the van will arrive. He knows when the chimes will sound. He is probably already at the window. He's always at the window. He loves to sit and watch, especially when there is any kind of raucousness on the street outside.

I never met him. I call him 'the old man', because that's how the woman who without fail visits him weekly, referred to him, when I ran into her one day in the hall. 'The old man,' she said, pointing towards the ceiling. 'I'm just making sure he's alright. He's not a problem, is he?' I shook my head and smiled—reasoning quietly that, since she was herself of considerably age, he must be quite old. I felt that I should ask about him, but got the impression that she had anticipated (and would have preferred to avoid) my inquiry, so I remained mostly silent.

After some small-talk, she left without my bringing-up the subject. The old boy is not a problem. He doesn't play loud music. He gets to bed early. Sure, he is heavy-footed at times. But in a world that could everywhere use some peace and quietude, his pottering around in the morning, is the least of anyone's problems. Indeed there are times when, were it not for the pounding of his cane, I wouldn't know whether he was dead or alive, no one would.

Any minute now, the chimes should begin: A few descending tones followed by a few ascending ones—a cadence; the descending tones again, then the cadence again. Silence. *Frankie! Frankie!* The children call the ice-cream man, Frankie. They called the previous ice-cream man Frankie, also. And when, some weeks ago, a rather flamboyantly-dressed young man wondered onto the street—if my memory serves me correctly—they teasingly called him Frankie, too. Their games are usually serious and silly, simple and complex, meaningful and meaningless—all at the same time. Presently, one group is defending the territory surrounding the open hydrant, which has become a sacred fortress or citadel of sorts. On its periphery, another group (war-paint and all) besieges them with assail after assail in a pitch battle. Water-cannons, squirt-guns, liquid-filled balloons, plastic buckets come into play; not to mention prolonged rasp-like death-throes and derisive laughter, and heckles and threats and cries. The sun is merciless. That the chimes are silent, that the van has not yet arrived, that Frankie even as the battle rages, might not be around the corner, but far away still, and may not arrive (not for a while yet, anyway) seems strangely suddenly, of little consequence, and no one's concern.

The old man sees more of the neighborhood than the rest of us (our house is at the high point of a hill, his apartment is the uppermost). His bed-room window at the rear of the building, affords him an unobstructed view of one

185

of the parallel streets (where the van makes its last stop before it rolls on to our own). He sees the children playing there. He sees the van as it arrives. He sees it as it leaves. This gives him the advantage of knowing before-hand when the bells are about to chime. (And since his mobility is restricted, he makes use of this head-start in order to get to the front window in time for the show.) Three descending tones played twice, now the ascending ones, descending again, followed by a pause or cadence; the entire phrase repeated, this time a little accelerando, followed by the finality of a sustained cadence. The chimes are sounding now. In ways different from yesterday, as tomorrow will be from today, a familiar scenario is being reenacted. The kid who cried is playful. The clogged drain is cleared. The older boy having complied with the grown-up who chastised him for riding his power bike when he knows there are younger children on the street, will be absent. The dog that acquired a taste for ice-cream, and barked incessantly wags now only his tail. The descending tones, the ascending tones, the cadence—the chimes are always the same. There are lyrics to the melody they play. They too will be unchanged. If only I could remember the lyrics! I have the feeling, that in a different time and at a different place, I sang them once. Sometimes I wake up in the middle of the night. Sometimes the words are on the tip of my tongue. One. Two. Three. I tap out the beat of a waltz, one two three! One two three! I'll improvise lyrics (nonsensical ones) which by the following morning, I will have forgotten, or will remember only the tempo, the one-two-three at which I sang them. One two three, one two three . . .

There are moments—bright moments—when in the furnace of a summer's day, things seem to be without reason, suddenly altered; time is twisted, each second lasts a minute, each minute seems into two or more inflated; for a while, the previous night's memories, the morning's melody—its half-remembered lyrics, its resounding cadences and tones—are juxtaposed; the here-and-now images and sounds, inextricably interwoven with those from God knows where, from God knows when. Tiny figures in a haze weightless and wind-borne appear, their voices and laughter, muffled; their shouts of, *Frankie!* quieted, one by one they retreat beyond the stoops and terraces and facades of their homes, leaving a spewing hydrant unattended, disputed territory abandoned, the sun by clouds obscured, the streets near-derelict. In a no-man's time unexplainable warp, an ice-cream vendor whose name might be Frank, and his companion, a stoic of a woman, stand now together motionless and silent amid the stacked cones, the dispensing machines and folded napkins. The last customer served, they sound the chimes once more. The giant eye-lid, of a horizontal hinged-window, that is access to their store on wheels, falls forward and closes. They start the engine. The van rolls uphill. It picks-up speed, it dances as it hits a bump in the road. It descends into a hollow. By the time it rises again, it will have, beyond our field of vision, vanished around a corner. Covering now slightly more rapid ground, it will appear again at a different time, on a different day, in a different place.

But it is not yet light. It is not yet day. And though sleep's dark hours are in months of summer shortened, they bury us deep still in dreams, dreams of yesternights and days, and of mornings not yet come; of chimes, of giddy laughs, and of children at play. When the sun rises, we will have forgotten; forgotten our dreams, forgotten always, some detail; failed to recognize an omen, to again incorporate into our regimen, the talisman, that would protected us from impending disaster, a catastrophe of which, we were, from so many dimensions, continuously warned. The unexpected floors us, takes us by surprise always, knocks us silly, hurls us back into the fluidity, the absurdity of dreams; dreams of a perfect day, a perfect existence, a perfect summer; even as the morning with its beauty and horror is upon us, even as gravity reaches up from inside the earth and restricts our movement, even as the tape of our lives dissolves and flashes from moments to moments-now; and, at birth again, rewinds, fast-forwards, and fades . . .

My day begins with a shuffle, with the faltering footsteps, the fragile feet of an old man journeying across the parched desert, the hills and crags of his years. He gets up early. He pounds the ceiling with his cane. He beats out a rhythm, he disentangles the cobwebs in his head. He rummages through the mementos of his past. He potters around. He flushes the toilet. He coughs. He drops his cane. He listens for the chimes, as he drinks his coffee. He hears the laughter of the children. He hums a tune he alone remembers. He loses his place in the melody. He drops his glasses, and just as easily manages without them. Yet despite the humidity, the oppressive temperatures, despite the thick, heavy, almost non breathable air, the noisy inconsiderate neighbors, their unruly kids and vicious canines; despite the rays of sunlight seeping through the blinds, the call to arms, as the ancient sacred city all but capitulates, under wave after wave of marauding invaders, the old man for some reason, even with the lateness of the hour, has on this morning, still not stirred.

How could a rag tag army of filthy barbarians assault a city so beloved and fortified! How could they! How could they thrash and trample in the manner that they did—all at the same time crammed into such limited space! It must be part of an elaborate ritual or ceremony. Fierce hordes! Rampaging in the thunder of a multitude, stained with the blood of innocents, they are getting closer, closer, closer! There are people up there! Not the thousands I imagined in my half-dream, but at least four or five sets of feet, I woke to discover, were milling around in the old man's apartment! There were people up there! Some-one with heavy boots was hurrying down the stairs. And when I looked out the window to see several official-looking vehicles double-parked in front of the building and a rather large man (the one no doubt who moments before descended the stairs) retrieving some sort of metal canister out of the trunk of one of them, I knew something terrible had happened. A woman was in the hallway, just outside my door. I recognized her voice. She was the woman with whom, in the spring, I had had the brief conversation—the one who periodically came to see the old man. I had no idea whom she was talking to, but she kept saying, 'Yes, sir,' as if some frightful formidable authority was admonishing her. Even before I went into the hallway, I got the impression that she was a lost soul. She reminded me almost of an actor arrived on set, only to discover his part written-out of an important script, his presence unacknowledged, his existence challenged. I opened the door. She was as white as a sheet. Then I noticed the cell-phone in her hand. Then I noticed the tears in her eyes.

'The old man?' I asked, when she was finished with her phone call—pointing towards the ceiling, in the same manner almost, that she had done the time we met before. But I already knew the answer. Somehow I already knew. She lifted a handkerchief to her face, and held it against her nostrils and mouth. Finally she spoke. 'Sometimes,' she said, 'when he is in a bad mood, he does not like to be bothered. And when he wouldn't open the door, I would still ask if he was alright and say something sweet to him. I did his laundry, you know! I always made sure he had something clean to wear. He'll come to the window, and I'd wave. This morning when he didn't answer, I had a funny feeling. I came back into the building. I knocked on the door again. I knocked on the door! I didn't know what to do! I called the landlord. I didn't know what to do!' She began to sob, and brought the handkerchief to her face once more.

After she left, I realized that I should have been a little more engaging (that I again had failed to tell her how I felt about the old boy). I started after her, but immediately ran into one of those officious looking, law-enforcer types. The front door was open. He was standing there. It was nearly seventy degrees; he was wearing a heavy coat. He smiled, and looked as if he wanted to talk to me. What I wondered first of all, was there under the present circumstances to smile about! Then I politely closed the door to my apartment, and decided never to go outside again.

September nights are extended long. The ice-cream van no longer comes around. The games the children play are different now; the foliage outside my window, not as dense. I sleep late. Of course one man's demise is another man's good fortune. That's the way things are. The old man's apartment is up for rent. Sometimes I think I hear him still. The wind rattles the panes in the window. Sometimes an eternity separates autumn's tender chimes from the tolls of winter, sometimes a single day, sometimes a moment. I look out into the night. I see clouds darkening the sky. Winter's heralds they are. Making up lyrics as I go along, I sing,

> *To all things*
> *All others are connected*
> *By one small thing*
> *How many are affected!*

Yet one man's life, his sojourn here on earth, is no more significant than a blade of grass, in the scheme of things; a blade of grass which grows, turns pale and is trod again into the earth from which it sprang; the grander spectacle hardly acknowledges him; his audience before the gods of Kosmos is brief, his role but minuscule; his footsteps pounding upon the ground, his lamentations and cries, but random decibels in time's upending symphony.

The star of all our beings put together, less-brightly burns than the most infinitesimal pin-point glow inside the impenetrable dark which surrounds us; no sooner lit, but flickers hardly, doomed already to be extinguished forever. And Kosmos, Kosmos itself, beyond and within, silent and indifferent, grand and far, mysterious and near— neither watches; neither watches, listens, waits, nor care; even as we clench our fist, even as we shed our tears; even as we pound our chest, walk on water, dance on air; beat a drum, or paint our face, or cry our woeful laughable cry:

> *Peaks of Himalya*
> *No sooner than we climb*
> *We'll journey to the stars*
> *And conquer what we find!*

I remember the words, the words to the melody, I remember them now! Frank, the ice-cream man, or whoever installed the chimes, had accidentally, or with purpose perhaps, left out a few crucial notes. That's what threw me off, that's what confused me. But I remember now. I remember. I was small. My mother was there. Someone sang to me. My father was ill. Someone sang and told me not to cry. Atop a tiny music-box, a ballerina danced and twirled, one two three! I remember now, she danced and twirled! One two three, go the bells of Saint One two three! Oranges and Lemons, Oranges and Lemons, go the bells of Saint One two three! One two three! One two three! *One two three . . .*

Made in the USA
Columbia, SC
27 May 2021

38616461R00115